THE STANTON PACK BOOK 4

KATHI S. BARTON

This is a work of fiction. Names, characters, places, and incidents are products of the author's imagination or are used fictitiously and are not to be construed as real. Any resemblance to actual events, locations, organizations, or persons, living or dead, is entirely coincidental.

World Castle Publishing, LLC
Pensacola, Florida
Copyright © Kathi S. Barton 2018
Paperback ISBN: 9781629899688
eBook ISBN: 9781629899695
First Edition World Castle Publishing, LLC, August 6, 2018
http://www.worldcastlepublishing.com

Licensing Notes
Cover: Karen Fuller
Editor: Maxine Bringenberg

Chapter 1

Hailey had a hundred and fifty or so miles to go today, but she had to rest. Even having help, loading the furniture had exhausted her. But she'd be home after lunch tomorrow. Or at least to the Stanton house. She looked over at David when he yawned.

"Not such a glamourous thing, helping people out, is it?" He grinned at her. She had come to like the kid after the four days they'd spent together. "I'm not sure about you, but I need a nice nap and some food. Not necessarily in that order either. How about you?"

"I could eat. You were telling me about the wolf pack that is going to take me in. Do you think they'll accept me?" She said sure—if not, they'd eat him. When he laughed, she did too. "They won't, right? Eat me, I mean."

"Not if you don't act stupid. And you don't strike me as being nearly as stupid as your father." He nodded but didn't laugh like she'd thought he might. "I'm sorry. I didn't mean to make fun of your father like that."

5

"No, It's all right. I think he's stupid too. I was just thinking about how much he hates my sister, Ray. Her name is Rachel, but no one calls her that but Grandma." He looked out the window, and she knew that he might be hurting. "The last time I saw my dad, he held me to his body with a knife to my throat to make Ray give him money. She did, and then had him arrested. The courts said that I could be with her and not my dad. My mom—she's dead now—she was a lush—Grandma called her that. She was drunk too much to care if I was hurt or not. As you can imagine, I've not had a good childhood. And don't get me started on my aunt—she's my dad's sister. She's fucking scary, pardon my language."

"That's rough. My parents split up when I was just a kid. Back then it was just me and my brother, Pete. His real name is Peter, after my dad, but he hates when I call him that." She laughed. "But I have two half-brothers and a half-sister from my mom. When it got to be too much with me living there too, I went to stay with Dad. Pete had already moved out by then."

None of that was true, she thought. Yes, she had a stepfather and the siblings, but she didn't care for any of them at all. And she'd not left, she'd been kicked to the curb. But telling people the truth made them act funny around her.

"My sister, Ray, she's really super nice. And she takes good care of me. And Grandma when she was alive. There was always money in the bank for us to use for food, bills, and stuff. I don't know what we would have done without her." Hailey asked him if he was ready to go eat. "I sure am. I think I could about eat a horse."

She was still laughing with him when they entered the restaurant. Her rig was parked in the lot and locked up tight. Also, and she'd not realized this when they started out, some of the pack was with them at all times. While she didn't mind the extra security, she wondered if it was necessary. Hailey asked them if they wanted to join her and David.

"No, ma'am. We're just fine. It might be better if we don't let people know that we're together. Might keep you and the boy safer." She didn't know what that meant about being safer, but nodded when he looked at David. "Thank you, though. It was nice of you."

David was hungry. But then, even when he wasn't *that* hungry, as he said, he could still out eat her. When he polished off the third hamburger and slurped the rest of his shake down, she asked him if he had hollow legs. His grin had her thinking that in a few years, women were going to be all over him. Even now, at sixteen, she thought he might be having some fun with it.

"My grandma used to say the same thing about me having hollow legs. I loved her so much. She was kind and knew all sorts of stories that made me laugh." She could see that he was still hurting from her passing. Hailey let him mourn her. She had no idea how to comfort someone when their relatives passed away. She didn't have any other than her dad and brother that she'd even shed a tear for. "What do you do? Or are you a trucker all the time?"

"I was when I was going to college—grad school. It was a way for me to make some money and pay for school too. Sometimes I'd miss a class or two, but I'd make it up. My mom didn't have any money for that, after she had her own kids to raise, as she called my step family." She was the one that looked out the window this time, thinking of the last time she and her mom had spoken. "I kept up my license in the event I'd have to do it again for some money. And so I have it. I work with my dad mostly, in the shop. We're outfitting a Mustang, the two of us."

"That's cool. My grandma had this Model T. She gave it to Colton too. I guess he's going to drive it back with him when they return. He let me drive it around the yard, then on the road for a little ways. It was amazing. And we laughed so hard. How much more do you have to go and get for them?" The change in subject was something that she was getting used to. He could change it quickly too.

Hailey told him that this was the last pickup as far as she understood. "Your grandma's house is probably torn down by now. The farmer that bought it, he wanted to get it planted soon. Your sister, Ray, what's the beef between her and your dad?" He said that he didn't know. That they were forever fighting. "Yeah, he doesn't strike me as the friendly type."

"Ray told me that you hit him in the face. I wish I could have seen that." She laughed with him. "He hurts me when he finds me. Then he makes me call Ray-Ray and tell her what he's done. I don't know why he'd do that. My sister would come and get me, take me to the hospital, then to a hotel for the night. After a while she got to keep me. My grandma said I could stay with her, she'd enjoy the company. And that she'd never tell Dad that I was there. Don't you think that's about the saddest thing in the world? To have to hide from your own dad?"

"Yes, but now you're safe, and that's all that matters, right?" He said that he guessed so. "All right. Do you want anything else? Or have you filled both legs up now?" He was still laughing when they were headed to the cash register.

Just before they were paying, Hailey looked up to see a man in a hoodie as well as a face mask entering the restaurant. It was fucking the last couple of weeks in June and hotter than hell, she thought. Hailey told David to get behind the counter.

As soon as he and the cashier were down and out of sight, the man in the mask started shooting up the ceiling. Hailey stayed by the counter. She wasn't going to move until David was safe and the man either dead or gone. Whatever he did, she had a feeling he was going to die unless he killed her first, which with her luck was a good possibility. When the robber looked at her, because she was sure that the cash was what he was there for, she smiled at him. He cocked his head and told her to go to the back of the restaurant with the rest of them.

"Nah, I don't think so. I just want to pay my bill here and leave. If you have a problem with that, we can discuss it, but I don't listen to people just because they say so." He pointed the gun at her head and she smiled at him again. "Killing me won't get you fuck, buddy, but a world of hurt."

"You think so? And what makes you so powerful that you can argue with a man with a gun?" She told him. "You want me to believe that you have some wolves in here? Right, lady. Get the fuck to the back of this place with the rest of the fuckers, and then you can go about your fucking way."

"You like that word, don't you? I met another man that liked to use it. It didn't do him much good either. I hit him in the face when he tried to give me shit." He frowned harder, and she smiled at him again. Hailey didn't so much as look at the two men behind him. But something must have spooked him because he turned. That was all that she needed, a moment to take action.

Hailey reached for her own gun and fired three times when he shot at one of the men who had changed to a wolf. When the gunman fell to the floor, she stood there for several seconds while her heart started to calm. Then she leaned over the counter and told the woman back there to call the police.

"Tell them that there was an attempted robbery and that the robber is dead. Shot by one of the patrons." She said that they wanted her name. "I don't know. A good citizen? See if they buy that."

Looking at the two wolves, she told them to get the hell out. When they were gone, she went to the back of the restaurant to see if the people there were all right too. None of them had been hurt, but they did thank her many times. Hailey wondered why there seemed to be so few when she'd thought the place was busy, but was too hyped up to care. David came to her then and hugged her tightly. Hailey hadn't realized how much she needed that.

The police arrived with a lot of noise and lights. When they came in the door, she was already on her knees with her gun out on one finger. In her other hand she had her license to carry. But that didn't stop them from cuffing her and sitting her on the curb in front of the small restaurant.

David was allowed to sit by her, but he wasn't to touch her. She was fine with that, and told him that he needed to call his sister. "She might see this on the news, and we don't want her to worry when there is no reason for it. Use the phone in my truck, and make sure you tell her that you're fine about a dozen times, all right?"

When he left her, with a police escort to her rig, she didn't move when the ambulance showed up to take the body. She had shot him three times, point blank; Hailey didn't think he was going to suddenly rise up and shoot anyone else. So taking him to the hospital seemed sort of dumb. But she wasn't in charge, so she sat there until they came to talk to her.

"The other people in the place, they said that you kept

him busy so that he'd not notice them leaving the back way."
She said that she'd not known that they were leaving, but had
noticed that there had seemed to be more people when they'd
entered. "You saved their lives. You know that, don't you?"

"Nah, he was just here to rob the place." She looked up at
the cop who had come out to talk to her. "He was, right? Only
there to rob the place? Come to think of it, he never mentioned
the cash register like I thought he would have."

"No, that wasn't his motive. We found a note on his person
that said that he wanted to go out with a bang, and that he was
going to out-kill—if you can believe that—what his own father
had done to put him in prison. I think he missed his daddy."
That sort of news did nothing to help her hold on to her lunch.
"You all right? You're looking sort of green."

"Such a charmer you are. Fuck no, I'm not all right. I just
killed a man." Another man came to stand by the first cop, and
she wondered what fucking branch he was from, dressed in a
pair of jeans and a shirt that had seen better days. She frowned
when he smiled at her. She wasn't charmed by him either. So
far there had been DEA, FBI, as well as the locals. She had no
idea what the fuck was going on.

The second man stood over her when the cop left. "My
name is Jules Stanton. I was hanging around here with a buddy
of mine when he got the call. I'd like to ask you a few more
questions if you don't mind. Just to help out." She asked him to
repeat his name. "My name is Julian Stanton, but I go by Jules.
Why?"

She peered up at him and laughed. "I don't suppose you're
a doctor, are you? Never mind—why wouldn't you be? Are you
perhaps related to—let me think of their names. Oh, right—
Colton Stanton, Levi Stanton, and a Wyatt Stanton? And there

was a woman...Tess. She helped me find the homes that I was dropping stuff off to when I was around there."

"They're my brothers." He was quiet for a moment, and she figured that he was checking with them. Hailey knew that they were cougars, but she didn't know if they were all in the same pride or pack. For all she knew, he might not live in the same area and this man had a different pride all together. "They said that you should have a young boy with you, David Spencer."

"I had him call his sister so that if this got to the news, she'd not freak out. Brother, huh? I've never met the other three, but I did your parents. I had dinner with them three nights ago. I'm Hailey Whitehead. My dad runs the auto repair place in Trinway." He told her that he'd only just gotten married and they'd been on their honeymoon until recently. "Figures. I don't suppose you could have them take this plastic shit off, could you? They're cutting into my wrists and it fucking hurts."

When he cut her loose, taking a knife from his boot to do it, she saw that she was bleeding pretty good. One of the straps that held her had cut deep into her skin. She was wondering if she should have it looked at when the man noticed it and freaked out.

"Holy fuck. Who put these on you that tight?" Hailey told him to keep his pants on, the first cops on sight were shook up a little. "They should have paid attention to what they were doing and not hurt the person that kept them from having a major clean up here."

"Nothing to it." Hailey looked at her wrist and was dizzy all of a sudden. It really was bleeding badly, but she just wrapped it up in her shirt tail. "How much longer am I going to be? I have to get some sleep, and then drive out tomorrow on the last leg of the journey to your brothers' houses."

She was getting dizzier by the second and felt the blood soaking her shirt. Looking down at it, she realized that she might just be in trouble here. When she heard her name being said, she didn't have the strength to even open her eyes.

~*~

Dane and the rest of the family stood up when Wyatt and his dad came from the operating room. The woman had been rushed here by helicopter, and Jules had asked that they come and care for her. When Wyatt said that she was going to make it, they all let out a breath. Dane hadn't been this nervous in a long time.

"The strap that they had tied her with cut deeply into her skin. The poor thing was cuffed well after they had cleared her, from my understanding. But it was the clip that did the most damage to her and opened her up to nearly bleed to death. Even after her skin opened up, the clip dug in deeper and cut not just her artery, but also some muscles. She'll be fine, but I'm worried that she'll be unable to use her hand as well as I'd like." Dane asked Wyatt if she could help her. She had all kinds of freaky abilities, but what she was thinking of to help the young woman was just a few drops of her blood. "I wish you would. But not a lot, okay? I don't want her to be sprouting wings or something when all she had was a very bad cut."

"I'm not making any promises." Dane walked down the hall with him as they went to recovery. "She saved all those people in the diner, they said, by killing the man that had come in to murder all of them. And look what was done to her. This is not right, on so many levels; you know that, don't you?"

"That's what Julian told me too. She's a pistol. When she was being prepped for surgery, she kept telling us that she was going to murder any mother fucker that messed up her tat. It

13

wasn't until we were almost done that I saw it. She's going to be pissed off." Dane laughed and looked at the young woman lying on the hospital bed. "David is safe, isn't he? She asked about him several times before we got her under."

"I was going to have them take him to the pack house until we can figure out where he'll stay. Colton said that he'd take him in as long as it was needed. That way the kid can make some extra money by helping him with the new furniture. Have you seen it yet?" Wyatt told her that he'd not. "Christ, it looks like the stuff was made just for that house. I mean, it's really gorgeous."

Stepping closer to the bed, Dane looked at the woman. She was pale, but it didn't diminish the fact that she was beautiful too. Her hair was as flaming red as she had ever seen, and her freckles—and there were a great many of them—stood out better with her being so washed out. Taking a knife from her boot, Dane made a small cut in her own finger and put it on Hailey's lips. It was the only bit of color on her except for her hair.

Nothing seemed to change about her, and Dane was worried. With the others, as soon as she gave them even a drop, they were different. Dane cut a deeper cut this time and let several drops of her rich blood drip into Hailey's open mouth as she held it open with her other hand. Wyatt asked her what she was doing.

"I don't think it's going to work on her." He asked her why and she told him. "Maybe she's not human after all. That's the only reason I can think of that would make her immune to what I am."

"She is. When we were working on her we could smell her better than we could if she wasn't bleeding out. She's wholly human." When nothing else happened, she asked Wyatt if she should give her any more of her blood. "I have no idea what she might do with what you've given her now. So go ahead, I guess. What can it hurt? Right?"

After giving her about a dozen more drops of her blood, the monitors over Hailey's bed started screaming. Dane was shoved out of the way as the crash cart was brought in and they started working on her. She had flatlined. Dane wasn't sure what she should do now. She had met the girl and liked her a great deal. Tess loved her too, as well as the rest of the family. Dane did not want her to die.

When they were readying the paddles to stabilize her, the machines suddenly stopped making any noise, but her heart rate however didn't seem to level out. She watched the monitors with everyone else. Whatever had happened, it had scared the shit out of all of them.

"Is she all right?" Wyatt said that she was for now and put his fingers on her wrist to take her pulse. "Do you think that I did it? Christ, I hope that I didn't make it worse rather than better."

"Look at her heart rate, Dane." She did, but didn't have a clue what she was looking for. "A normal heart rate for a female is sixty to one hundred beats per minute. But since she's in very good shape and probably lifts weights and runs, it should be about seventy or below at a rested state. Lower if she were training."

Dane understood now and saw that her heart rate was well over two hundred. She looked at Wyatt when he turned the monitor off. Backing away from the bed with him, she was almost afraid to ask him what the fuck was going on with her. She was glad then that no one else had noticed her heartrate or that Wyatt had turned off the machine. He did explain to them that the machine wasn't working right, and that seemed to satisfy them all. But not her. She was afraid.

"She's changed." Dane asked him into what. "I have no idea, but it concerns me a good bit. I've never met her, but I have a feeling that she is going to be very fucking pissed off. And I have no idea what to tell her when she asks, either." Wyatt looked like he was concerned, and she was as well. None of the others, not any of them, had reacted like Hailey had. "I'm going to sit with her for a while and send the staff away to get a break. While they're gone I'm going to check her wrist. I have a feeling that it's healed."

She didn't want to stay but Dane had to know. If she had done something to this woman, she was going to be the one to tell her. Watching as the staff left the recovery room, she wondered what her own heart rate was, and nearly screamed when Brayden asked her if she was all right.

Yeah, I'm fine, but this woman might want to kill me when she wakes up. After she told him what she'd done, he was quiet for a few moments. *I'd feel so fucking much better if you tell me what you're thinking.*

I haven't any idea what to think, to be honest with you. I mean, she could be just about anything, right? Dane told him that she could be everything too. *We all are, aren't we?*

No, none of you are everything like me. You don't have the ability to change into something without a heartbeat. You also can't blend into the colors around you, like become invisible. There are a few other things, too, that none of you can do that I can. I'm afraid I've made her exactly like me. Brayden said that he still wasn't sure what to think, and she told him that she'd talk to him in a little while. *Wyatt is going to check her wound out to see if she's healed now that*

16

his staff is gone. Brayden, I know this woman. She is going to be very pissed off when she finds out.

We'll deal with it like we do everything else. By the way, the police came by and they're picking up her hospital tab. And the man who put the cuff like straps on her has been put on administrative leave without pay. He nearly killed her, and they aren't taking that too well. She told him that was what she'd do too. *I understand but he can't afford to be off work for very long. Dad is going to see if he can help out while they investigate and see if Hailey is going to press charges. If she does, then he's done.*

Dane couldn't feel sorry for the man. He had hurt Hailey badly. And even if he had put them on her when everything was going down, that was no excuse. While admitting that he might have put them on her too tightly, it didn't negate the fact that she'd been hurt badly enough to have almost died. The man should have been paying more attention to his captive.

When Wyatt was finally able to cut away the gauze and cast that was holding her arm still, she knew by the look on his face that she was healed. Taking the necessary steps forward to look, she wasn't surprised to see that not only was she healed, but her tat, a small butterfly, was perfect as well.

"Now what?" Wyatt said that he'd make arrangements to get her out of the hospital. No one needed to know about this. "She can come to our house. I'll take care of her."

"I'd rather she went with my parents. Just because Dad can help her if something goes wrong with this. I haven't any idea what it might be, but he's got all that equipment in the lower levels of his house, so he could take care of her if she codes again." Dane said that she could see that. "All right. I'm going to make arrangements here. You go out and tell them what we're going to do. If you don't want to mention the blood that you gave her to them, tell me now and I'll not mention it to the family. Nor to the hospital staff."

"I think we're going to have to, don't you?" Wyatt nodded and grinned. "Christ, what the fuck are you finding so funny about this?"

"She's not my mate." It took Dane a minute to figure out what he was saying. "If she's one of the others' mates, I cannot wait for them to tangle with her. The few minutes we did when she was brought in, she sounded just like you."

"Well, that's a good thing, right?" He burst out laughing as he put on fresh gauze and the cast. She watched him as he methodically put it around her wrist and then taped it. "You think that she'll be one of the others' mate, Wyatt? I mean, that would be awesome, but scary too."

"I have no idea, but she's going to be a handful. Just hearing her barking orders in here when they brought her to us, I could have sworn that she was already a part of our family." He looked at her with panic in his eyes. "Christ, you don't think that my mate will be a ball buster, do you?"

"I hope so."

When she left him there with terror in his eyes, she was laughing until she got to the others. David was there now, and it looked as if he might have been crying. When Allie hugged him, she knew that the kid was going to be all right. Dane told them everything, including what she'd done to bring her to this point.

Chapter 2

Hailey opened her eyes then shut them again. She had no idea where she was or how she'd gotten there. Opening her eyes again, she sat up and glanced around the room, and then laid back down.

"What the fuck kind of hospital is this?" The voice startled her when she answered her, and Hailey looked at Lucy Stanton. Hailey had not noticed her when she'd been looking around. "What do you mean, this isn't a hospital? I passed out. I vaguely remember the ride to one. They took me in a chopper."

"Yes, well, things progressed faster than they thought they would." Hailey sat up and asked about David and her dad. "Your dad has been here several times, but we sent him home this morning to rest up. David is fine. He's living with the pack right now until we figure out the situation with you."

"What sort of situation is there with me?" When Lucy sat down in the chair next to the bed, Hailey got nervous. "Am I going to prison?"

"Why on earth would you think that?" She told her that

19

she'd killed a man. "Yes, well, you did become a hero to a great many people for that as well. I don't think you have to worry about prison. Not unless you cause more trouble. You're not, are you?"

"I have no idea. And don't think I didn't notice that you changed the subject. What is the situation with me?" Lucy was anxious, which was making Hailey more nervous. But when something seemed to skid over her skin, she shivered. "Where am I? I'm assuming that this is your home and not the hospital that I thought they were taking me to."

"You were there for a while. And operated on there as well. My son, Wyatt, did the surgery to repair the damage that was done to you when that man put the plastic cuff things on too tightly. But you're fine now." She looked at her wrist and saw that there wasn't a thing wrong with her. "You've been healed."

"I don't believe in witch doctors. Nor do I think that if one of you licked it or something that it would be this clean of a tear in my skin." She looked at Lucy. "I don't want to be rude here, but I'm freaking the fuck out. What the hell is going on?"

The door opened and there stood Dane and Tess. Allie came in right behind them, and she had a feeling that they were there so someone wouldn't be hurt by her. Getting up, she realized that she had on a man's shirt as well as heavy socks. Pulling the socks off, she asked where her clothing might be.

"In the bathroom. Lying on the sink. I hope you don't mind, but they've been laundered as well as the stains removed." Hailey made her way to the bathroom when it was pointed out to her, and stripped off the man's shirt on the way. "You aren't shy, are you, my dear?"

"We all have the same parts, so no, I'm not shy. Why am I here, and why am I getting the run around about answers?

20

Start with how long I've been here." Tess told her four days. "Okay. And I know that my dad and David are all right. But I'm to understand that there is a situation with me. I want one of you to tell me. Right now, if you don't mind. I'm not dealing with the unknown as I have in the past. Probably because I'm trying my best to be polite. But I won't be any more if someone doesn't talk."

When she thought about her shoes, she realized that at some point she must have pulled them on. Reaching for the shirt while they were trying very hard not to look at her, she pulled it over her head and realized that she had on her bra. Hailey thought that she'd decided not to wear it and must have put it on anyway. There was something going on with these people, and they weren't going to tell her.

Sitting down on the bed, Hailey couldn't believe how great she felt. She supposed that having four days of sleep would do that for a person. When Allie asked her how she was feeling, Hailey asked her how she was supposed to feel. Of course, no one answered her.

"Look, this is getting us nowhere and it's pissing me off. Either tell me what is going on, or I'm going home. This is bullshit." Lucy huffed at her. "I'm sorry, but between the four of you, you'd think that one of you could tell me what the fuck is going on."

"When you were in the hospital, I went to see you. You had lost a lot of blood, and Wyatt, who had operated on you, thought that you'd not have much use of your hand that he'd worked on. So I asked him if I could help you." Hailey looked at the other women as Dane continued. They were smiling, but they were tight smiles. "I've been enhanced. I was in a medical lab where I was given all kinds of different drugs to see if they would kill me. In the process of that, I was changed into what I am now."

"Okay, bully for you. What does that have to do with me?" Dane got up and went to the window. "You're stalling. Just fucking tell me already."

"I gave you a lot of my blood. Perhaps a quarter of a cup. I didn't want you to be hurt just because you saved a bunch of strangers." Hailey looked at the women again and they were all avoiding looking at her. This time, it pissed her off.

"What is wrong with me? I have a feeling that I either have two heads that are going to sprout soon, or you're telling me that I'm as enhanced as you are." Dane nodded. "I don't understand. You mean I have a second head. Because you are so not telling me that you fucking changed me into another being. I'm a fucking human that has enough shit going on in her life—I don't need this too."

"I'm afraid that you're changed." She looked at Lucy now that she was speaking. "I'm sure that Dane didn't mean to do that to you. She was only trying to help you so that you'd not be handicapped."

"So now, instead of having something wrong with my wrist, I'm wholly changed into something else. Is that about right?" Lucy nodded, as did the rest of the women. "Fuck this shit—take it back."

"I can't. And even if I could, the change has already altered your body and DNA." Hailey stood up, then sat back down. It was too much, and when Dane spoke again, she sat there. "I don't know the extent of what you can do. But I have a feeling that you're exactly like I am. Every part of you is something new."

Hailey stood up again and walked to the door. She had no

idea what to say to these women, but she had to get out of there before they told her that she could shift into something. As she ran down the stairs she saw Denny with two men, and realized then how much they all looked like their father—the sons that she'd met, anyway. He asked her where she was going in such a hurry.

"Home. And don't come around, either. I don't want to see any of you." The man standing next to his father started toward her. "You try and detain me, and I'll put you in a world of hurt. I'm not in the mood to fuck around with you."

"There's something else you should know."

She told him to shut the fuck up and went out the front door. She was nearly to the garage when she saw her rig. Hailey had no idea how it had gotten there but was glad that it was. Getting into it, she hoped the fuck it had been unloaded, because she wanted nothing else to do with these people.

Hailey cried all the way home. She was overwhelmed and stressed, and she hated to cry. But it was too much. She had been changed; into what, she had no idea. Hailey hated that someone had it taken upon themselves to do this to her. Didn't they realize that she had enough going on...? Okay, probably not, but that didn't change the fact that they had changed her.

By the time she was pulling her rig into the back lot of her dad's shop, she'd gotten some control over herself. Not that she was any less pissed off, but she wasn't going to let it affect or change her life. If she ignored it, maybe it would fade out or something. But Hailey had a feeling that she was stuck this way.

Taking a shower made her feel better—and changing out of the clothing that she'd been in. Hailey threw them in the trash, even her tennis shoes. While she was standing in front of her closet, she was thinking of what to put on when she was suddenly dressed.

"Mother fuck balls and save the queen." She fell on her ass and looked at the shoes and jeans she had on. Looking again, she realized she was wearing a shirt, jeans, shoes, and bra that she'd never seen before—the bra was a pretty blue one that looked good with her shirt. Lying down on the floor, she tried to tell herself that she'd dressed and forgotten. "Yeah, like that fucking is going to make you feel better. You didn't hit your head girl, you had your wrist cut."

When someone knocked on her bedroom door, she actually screamed. Her dad, just on the other side, asked her if she was all right. Fuck, she had no idea. But she wasn't going to tell him that.

"Yeah, I'm fine. Just startled myself, that's all." Boy, was that an understatement. "I'll be out in a bit. I need to clean up after myself. How is the back and hand?"

"Fine, fine. You come on out and we'll have us a nice lunch. I've missed you being around here." She wanted to cry again, but knew that tears would get her nowhere. "Oh, there was a news crew here yesterday to ask you what it feels like to be a hero."

Getting up, she opened her door and smiled at her dad. He had been her rock, even before she'd come here to live with him. Hugging him, almost afraid to think about anything else that might happen, she talked about the trip and how much she'd enjoyed driving again.

"Dad, if you don't mind, just tell the news people, whoever they are, that I've left and you don't foresee me returning." He said that he'd thought she'd say that and had already started telling them. "Thank you so much, Dad."

"You thinking of going on the road again?" She nodded,

thinking that was the best way to not have the Stantons coming over and talking to her anymore. "There's some pizza left over from last night if you want that. I'm going to have me a salad with some tuna on it."

While she heated up the pizza and opened the can of tuna for him, she half listened while he told her how much better he was feeling now that she was home again. Sitting down with him as he dumped tuna all over the greens that he liked, she asked him if the other men were working out. The ones from the pack that had been sent over.

"Oh yes, they really are." He took a few bites of his salad, and she knew he was avoiding telling her something. She told him to spill it. "Your stepfather called here. What a nasty man he is. He wants to talk to you about something. I'm sure that it's another loan, aren't you?"

"Yes. They're not going to get anything from me, Dad. I told him that the last time. When you lend someone money, you expect some return on it. Not that they asked, but just took the cash, but I would like to have it back. So they still owe me about ten grand from that loan and the last two. No more. I swear it." Dad gave a long whistle and asked her if they'd told her what it was for. "Yeah, to catch up on their bills. It's always the same thing. I'm not supporting them. They kicked me out when their new family started coming along. And Mother told me not to come sniffing around them again. It's always them that do the sniffing and taking."

"I'm sorry as I've ever been about what they did to you. You and her, you don't even speak, and I can't say I blame you either. But this is more than about the money, isn't it? Howard is the only one that calls here. Do I need to have a talk with her?" Hailey shook her head and said that it was fine. "No, I don't think it is. You should tell me so that I can have my speech ready when he calls here again."

She played with her pizza, trying to tell her sweet father what had been done to her. Before she could figure it out, someone rang the doorbell in the front of the house and he went to answer it. Hailey got up to dump her food in the trash, no longer hungry. The man that came in with her dad looked as if he was going before a firing squad.

"I'm Colton Stanton." She asked him why he thought that she'd give a good fuck. Her dad told her to behave. "I've come to have a talk with you about a few things. You left my parents' home before I got to tell you something."

"Fuck that shit. I've had about enough talking to your family. Go away." He looked at her dad and asked if he could have a moment with her. "No, don't leave, Dad. This is your home. He's the one that needs to get out of here." But he left anyway, leaving her in the room with another fucking Stanton.

"You're my mate, Hailey." She stood there for a full minute before she burst out laughing. It wasn't really funny, but it was either laugh or throw a very unladylike hissy fit. And she was leaning harder and harder toward having one. "I wanted to tell you before you left the house. But you didn't stop."

"And you didn't think that was a clue for you to stay the fuck away from me? Holy Christ, could this day get any worse?" He grinned at her and she glared back. "Okay, you've told me what you wanted to. It's time you go back to your nutball of a family."

"If you know anything about my kind, you know that I can't do that." Hailey slid to the floor, unable to take much more today. "I would really like to talk to you. I know that you've been told about the blood and all."

Her dad asked what was going on, that he'd heard her laughing and came back in. "Shit for brains here is my mate. And I may or may not be this freakazoid from hell that can do all kinds of shit that I didn't ask for, nor did I want. I'm healed, woo hoo. And I killed a man in a diner. I'm sure that I'm missing something in all this, but— Yes, I've had my wrist cut—again, not anything that I wanted." She looked at her dad. "That about sums up my day—how about yours?"

Dad was still laughing as he went out the door again. He said something about mates and trannies, but she chose not to hear it. Colton sat down at the table where she'd been earlier. Hailey tried to think beyond her morning so far to what the fuck she was going to do now.

"Are you all right?" Hailey just glared at him. "Okay, wrong thing to ask. Is there anything I can do for you, other than leave?"

The phone rang, and she decided that she didn't want any more shit piled on her today. When Colton asked if she wanted him to answer it, she waved him off. She heard the chair scrape and him talking on the phone as he came back to where she was.

"It's your father." She told him to tell him to fuck off if it was Howard, because her dad was in the garage. Colton nodded and spoke into the phone again. "Mr. Whitehead, I'm assuming? I'm afraid that your daughter isn't in a position to talk to you right now." Howard must have corrected him. "Oh, pardon me, Mr. Damon. But the situation is the same—she cannot speak to you right now."

Colton pulled the phone away from his ear and she could hear Howard screaming to put her on the phone. When she told Colton to give her the phone, she listened for Howard to take a breath before she tore into him.

"Listen to me, you mother fucker. I told you that there isn't going to be any more funding of your fucking shit. You go out, find a fucking job, and leave me the hell alone. I'm not now, nor am I ever, going to loan you money again. And you can tell Mother dearest if she doesn't pony up on what she already owes me, I'm fucking going to take her to court." Howard told her to shut the fuck up and hand over some cash or else. "You aren't getting another dime out of me until you pay me the ten grand that you already owe me. And even then, I'm not going to hand over anything to either of you. Get a fucking job, like I suggested to you over four years ago. I don't live there anymore, thanks to you and Mother, so there isn't any reason at all that I can think of for paying you anything."

He might have been saying something else, but she disconnected the call. While she sat there on the floor Hailey started to cry. Fuck, this was a fucker of a day. She looked at Colton when he took the phone from her and turned the volume down. Hailey didn't bother getting up. She thought she'd stay right there for the rest of her life.

~*~

In the few minutes that he'd been there, Colton knew a great deal about his mate. She was overwhelmed, for sure, but she was also somewhat defeated. For now, he thought. In a few minutes, he just knew she was going to bounce back from this and be fine, for a little while anyway.

When she continued to sit there, tears rolling down her cheeks, his cat wanted him to comfort her, but he thought they both might live longer, him and his cat, if he stayed right where he was. While he didn't know her yet, the conversation that she'd had with her stepfather was enough for Colton to know that she didn't suffer fools.

"To give you several hundred thousand reasons this won't work with us, I have a deadbeat stepfather and a mother from hell, as you heard. I used to live with them when I was younger. At least I did with her. Then Howard moved in, not six months after she left my dad, and it was announced that she was going to have a baby. That was about fifteen years ago now, and the oldest is about that age. My biological brother, who is older than me by about eight years, lived here with Dad when she left him. I was just a kid. The thought of my mother having a baby was crazy to me." Colton asked her how many other siblings she had. "Just my brother, Pete. He and my dad have the same name. But I have two half-brothers and a half-sister that are, if not worse than, as bad as the parents are. When I was fourteen, I came home from college and she had all my things packed up and to the side of the road. Some of it was being picked over by others, as she told me that I wasn't going to be living with them anymore. They had enough mouths to feed. Even though they were both getting welfare for me as well as the other three by then. And I hadn't asked them for a single thing in all that time. Even paying my own way through college."

Colton decided to skip over the part where she told him that she had been at college at fourteen, and slid to the floor too—just to be able to talk to her without straining his neck, he told himself. She pulled her gun out of her pocket and laid it on the floor next to her. He had a feeling that she wasn't threatening him with it, but more like it was uncomfortable the way she was sitting.

"I'm a Doctor of Psychology. I have a practice here in town, and I also consult for the police department, both state and local, when they need me. I don't want to psychoanalyze you, but I think you're very stressed right now." She snorted at him and he nearly laughed. But again, he was trying to live as long as he could and not die by his mate. "Would you like to go out to dinner with me?"

"No." He laughed then, and she looked at him again. "What is your deal, Dr. Stanton? I mean, I couldn't have been clearer about us not coming together as mates. In the event that you might have missed some of this shit, I'm having a terrible day, and if you fuck with me right now, I might end up going to prison. At the very least jail for killing your ass."

"I'm not trying to add to it, I swear, but I can help you with a bit of it." She asked him how the fuck he was going to do that. "Well, will you go out to dinner with me? I promise you on my mother's heart that I will do nothing untoward to you. I won't try and hold your hand or steal a kiss when you're not looking."

"I can dress myself." He wasn't sure what she meant until she spoke again. "I was in my room just now, out of the shower and wearing a towel, and thinking about what I was going to wear to help my dad. And then I had on the exact thing I'd been thinking about. Something that I did not own before this. This is some of the freaky shit I'm dealing with right now. And going out to dinner with you isn't something that is going to take any of this stress away."

"May I tell you a few things about what you might be able to do? I've been living around Dane for a few months now, and she can do some things that scare me a little too." She didn't answer him, so he went ahead with his thoughts. "She can make her hand morph into anything. A blade or a gun. Anything that she might need. Can you?"

"Are you fucking kidding me?" He told her that he wasn't

30

known to have a sense of humor. "I don't want to be able to morph my hand into anything but my hand. Next thing you'll tell me is that I can shift into anything too."

He just stared at her, not looking away when her stare became uncomfortable. She asked him if he was saying that she really could shift into anything. Nodding, he watched her as she stood up, grabbed her gun, and moved out. Or really what she did was bounce to her feet. Getting up too, he followed her out to a garage that was as foreign to him as if she'd been in a space ship.

Her dad was bent over a car engine and singing off tune to music that was probably as old as he was. When Hailey asked him what he wanted her to do, Colton sat down on a chair and waited and watched her. He had nothing else to do today, having taken the week off to get his house in order, so he thought that he could wait until she settled. For some reason, he thought that she'd work this out without his help.

Christian asked him through their link if he was all right. *So far. I don't think she's going to be easy about any of this. Can you do me a favor? Have Dane look up a family by the name of Howard Damon. I have a feeling that they don't live around here. But that's her stepfather and her mother. Hailey and her other family do not get along at all.*

Watching Hailey, Colton had an opportunity to see her work. And bend over. He wasn't spying on her, but she had a lovely form when she was bent like she was. He was just wondering if she would wear a dress for him when she turned and caught him looking at her. Instead of saying anything to him, Hailey went to the other side of the car she was working on so that he couldn't see her.

That was too easy. And if she's related to these deadbeats, she is

31

well to be away from them. Dane was talking now, and he asked her what was going on. *About a year ago, give or take, they filed for bankruptcy. And it was down to the final part, just waiting on the check, when your mate there called the courthouse and gave them some vital information. Like the fact that she hasn't lived there for the over a decade, and they were still getting money for her even though she didn't live there. It took her all of five minutes to send them all the paperwork that had her established at her father's home, paperwork on how she had been taking care of her own bills, as well as college, without their help at all. Apparently, that was on the application, that they were so behind since they'd paid her tuition. As you can imagine, that did not go over well. They now have to pay the money back that they received from the state to house and feed her. The loan was voided, and in addition to having to pay back what they got, they are never to receive any help from any agency. Ever. I like that, by the way, that she isn't a push over.*

She said that her mother owes her ten grand. Does Hailey have that much? Dane whistled in his head. *I take it she has a lot.*

Your mate is one smart cookie. Graduated from high school and college just a few months later. She was fourteen at the time. Working on things like Brayden does while she finished her education by getting a doctorate in two subjects. The things she makes, hers are bigger — more of things like the grocery cart that has a lift on it to raise the person up to reach the higher items. Also, it says here that she invented a way for bags, the paper ones, to be biodegradable faster than they can be now. He asked Dane if she'd been paid well. *Very well. While she's not on the same level that you guys are, she's made herself a very comfortable living with it. You might be interested to know that she's a lot smarter than she lets people see. She has a PhD in language arts, whatever the hell that is, as well as one in mechanical engineering. If you don't marry her, I might.*

When Hailey started cursing, Colton went to her. Her father did as well, but he was also picking up the first aid kit as he made his way to her. Before Colton or her father got to her, she put her hand behind her back and said that she was fine, just a little scratch. But Colton could see that she was freaking out again. When her dad told her to be careful, Colton made his way to her slowly.

"Let me see." He was quiet, and knew that her dad wouldn't be able to hear them because of his music. "Let me see where you might have been cut."

"It's gone." He figured that was what had happened. "I sliced my hand open because I wasn't paying attention, and it sealed up on its own."

Colton took her hand into his and saw how badly she was shaking. He looked over her hand and then turned it over to look at the other side. She was right—there was nothing there to indicate that she'd ever hurt herself. When she jerked from him and stepped back, he did as well. She was as skittish as a newborn colt.

"What are you still doing here, anyway?" She bounced back reasonably quickly, and he couldn't help but smile at her. "You're not at all my type. I want you to get into whatever you came here in and leave me alone. I'm not having a great day, and you're not helping me. I need to concentrate on what I'm doing. Please? I just can't take too much more today."

He left her there. He didn't want to, but Colton could see that she really was trying her best to deal with things. Making his way out to his car through the house, he put one of his business cards on the table, along with his personal number on the back. Colton figured that it would be in the trash before he was home. But he'd be back. And soon.

How you doing? He told Dane he was heading home, that Hailey was too stressed out to deal with anything else. *I'd say that's a fair statement. I've been digging deeper. The first day she was here, she told me not to investigate her. I told her that I only believe about half of the little that I'd found. She said that it was probably all true. If you're driving, you might want to pull over for this.*

He was sitting in her driveway and told Dane that. *I have a feeling that you're building up to something and I'm not going to like it.* She told him he more than likely wouldn't.

Colton, why don't you come here before going home? Please. I think this is something that I need to show you rather than just tell you. He asked her again what it was. *Just come here. Please, Colton. You might have more than your hands full with her.*

All right. But I have to tell you, Dane, this girl isn't like any other that I've dated. She's strong, opinionated, as well as smart. And she's nice. She didn't say anything. *Are you going to break that illusion that I have of her?* Dane told him, again, to just come to her house. Colton thought that was scarier than her telling him what it was.

Chapter 3

She made dinner for her and her dad. He was supposed to be on a diet — he had type two diabetes, and the doctor had told him that if he lost weight, he might not need to take the medication any longer, but he would definitely live longer. So they were both having a grilled chicken salad without crackers or croutons. And his dressing would be lite, and hers would be too. For him. When Dad came into the house, wiping his hands dry, she heard the phone ring in the other room.

"Your mom and Howard been calling you?" She told Dad that there were eleven messages, but that she thought some of them might be for him. "She just doesn't give up, does she? I tell you, Hailey, had I known that she was more than someone just sleeping around when I divorced her, you would never have stayed with her. Every day, I'm sorrier than you can think about that."

"I know, Dad, but there isn't anything we can do about that now. Let's just eat." He finished washing his hands, this time with the antibacterial soap, and she cut up the grilled chicken.

Neither one of them could cook, but she could put something on the grill if she had to. That was why they usually had salads. It was easier to clean up and it was good for them. "I was thinking of going back on the road again, like I told you earlier. Just to get away from the phone calls and the threats. You know as well as I do that they're not going to quit. And if I'm not here, you won't be singled out either."

"Which one of them is threatening you, honey? That mom of yours or Howard?" She said that it was mostly Howard, but Mom had been on there as well. "That man of yours, does he know about what she did to you?"

"No, but I'm pretty sure that he'll find out soon enough. And he's not my man and never will be." Dad nodded as he ate his dinner. "They have this woman there, one of the Stantons. She's pretty smart, and I'm thinking that since I'm supposed to be a mate to one of them, she's searched pretty hard for everything."

"You should explain it to them. At the very least that man. He should know what you did." She told Dad that she didn't really want to talk about that man or her mom. "I'm just saying, baby. If that's the reason you're going back out, you do know that if you have someone to support you both mentally and physically, you'd be better off than just trying to deal with this on your own."

Hailey pushed her salad away. She'd not been all that hungry anyway. Dad said that he was sorry that he'd ruined her meal, and she said she'd been feeling off. He didn't believe her any more than she would have if it had been him saying it.

"I don't want a mate, Dad. I have seen what happens to married couples. And while I'm not stupid enough to think that all marriages are like yours, I still have no desire to have a man around telling me what to do." Hailey looked at her dad. "I mean, having you around is hard enough on my poor old body."

They were both laughing as she got out the fruit salad. Dad couldn't have much of it, but they both enjoyed it. When he took his bowl of it, she pushed around her own fruit in the bowl while she thought about everything.

"I was hurt after I killed that man. I'm sure that you knew that." He said that he did. "Well, after the operation, or sometime after, Dane gave me a little too much of her blood to heal me, I guess. The problem was, she was enhanced at Nelson's." Dad dropped his fork and looked at her. "She believes that I will be like her. Everything that she can do, so can I. Because of what they did to her at Nelson's. I've been wondering if she would have bothered had she known about me and the company."

"What are you going to do about it?" She said she wasn't going to do anything. "Honey, you know as well as I do that because of Nelson's, even if they're gone, there will be someone that will come for you again. To be honest with you, I wondered why no one has so far."

"Yeah, me too." She got up to wash the dishes, and while the water was filling up in the sink, she showed him what she knew about herself so far. "I can heal myself. Or at least my body does. And I can do this."

She put out her hand and watched as it morphed into a long slim blade. Then she had it turn into a chainsaw, as well as a hammer. When she looked at her dad, he didn't say anything, but he was scared. Not of her, she hoped, but what was going on.

"Anyone else know about this?" Hailey told her dad that the Stantons more than likely did. "You're also thinking that

37

they know that you were the one that invented the equipment that they used out there, aren't you, honey? You said that was going to bite you in the ass someday."

"I never sold it to them, but it's doubtful that anyone is going to care about that. I helped them, in a big way, to create the monsters that they made out there. And Dane and whoever else might have been there at the same time." She sat back down on the chair after turning off the water. "Dad, I have to get out of here. If I don't they're going to bring this up again, and I'll get you into trouble. You've only just gotten to the point where you want to hire others to help you out. If the town finds out what I did, then they're going to quit using you altogether."

The phone rang again, and she ignored it. Dad got up, however, and answered it. When he changed his tone and laughed, she figured it was one of his old cronies and finished the dishes, then went to her room. Hailey decided that she could pack up and be gone in the morning. There wasn't any point in hanging around here until the paper got wind of this shit.

The knock at her door woke her. Hailey hadn't realized that she'd fallen asleep, and told her dad to come on in. When Colton was there, she got up off her bed and moved to the other side of the room away from him.

"I've come to talk to you." She didn't know if his voice was different with anger or not. She didn't want to get to know him that well either. When he came in her room and closed the door, Hailey asked him what he thought he was doing. "I want to talk to you about some things. Dane did some deeper digging, and I want to talk to you about it."

"You mean before you go to the newspaper? I'd rather you waited until I was gone first. My dad can't afford to take a hit on his business. Well, he could, but he likes what he does, and

38

there isn't any point in him being—"

"Why do you think I'd go to the newspaper?" Hailey asked him if he'd figured out what she'd done with Nelson's. "Yes, that's what I wanted to talk to you about. But I'm not going to the newspaper. What do you think I'd tell them about you?"

"Would you like to know what the papers said about me before? Here, let me get it for you." She got out the box that she'd put all the newspaper articles in about her and what she'd done to help Nelson's murder people. "It's all there. I was called a whore for making that equipment for them. That one I never understood, but that's what they said the public was calling me. It was my equipment, but I didn't make it for them, but for hospitals. I couldn't help who bought it after it went into production."

Reaching into the box, she pulled out the first slip of newspaper. She read the headlines off it. "Local woman helps Nelson's." There were more, and when she got to about the fourth or fifth one, he grabbed her hand and told her to stop.

"They ruined everything that I worked for. The papers put in there that I had invented those machines just for them to use to create monsters. That I had worked hand in hand with the men and women out there and made myself a millionaire. I was wealthy before I found a way for the DNA of several people to be mixed together to help make stronger skin for burn victims, so I never got that either. It was for people that had been cut up in an accident to be helped, and not scarred for the rest of their life. It wasn't my idea to use it for what they did."

"I never thought it was." She stared at him and he asked her to have a seat. "I know that they ruined you, but it didn't stop you, did it? You went on to invent more things to help others, and even put a patent on a great many of your projects so that something like this couldn't happen again."

"I don't know what you're talking about." But she did. And if Dane was good enough to find out about her patents, then she also knew what name she was using to disassociate herself from the inventions in some way. Looking at her hands, she told him that she could morph her hands into objects. "I showed my dad. I *know* that he won't tell anyone."

"Neither will I or my family." She didn't say anything. Hailey knew people and what they'd do for a just a dime. "I don't need the money, and even if I did, I'd still never do anything like that to you."

"You say that now, but what if they come to you with this amazing deal? You'll cave then too. Everyone does." He asked her who had betrayed her. "Everyone and anyone that knew about it. My own mother is blackmailing me, along with that fucker Howard. Even my professors at college. They were thinking at one time to take away my doctoral for my involvement in this. But because of the fact that their name was never mentioned in any of the articles, they magnanimously told me that I could retain it, but they'd be keeping an eye on me."

Hailey got up and started packing the rest of her stuff she was going to take with her. She didn't say anything when he asked her where they were going, but pulled her duffle out and packed her things in it. Taking it to her rig, Hailey was making a list of shit that she'd need to take with her when he joined her in the living area in the cab.

"Go away." He said that he couldn't do that. "Well, you and my dad have a really good time while I'm gone. Because I'm leaving in the morning."

"I have to gather up some things to take with me. And to

make arrangements with my patients." She asked him what he thought he was doing. "I'm going with you. I told you, you're my mate, and I can't be without you, even if you're pissed at me all the time."

"Don't you fucking get it? I don't want a mate. And I certainly don't want one that is going to be dragged into this shit. They're relentless when it comes to getting information, and then they don't even say anything that is remotely truthful. I'm not going to be here when the paper finds out." She found herself on her back on her bed with him over her. "Get the fuck off me."

"Not until you listen to me. Fuck, but you're stubborn." His body was lying over hers, but it wasn't sexual. At least it didn't feel that way. "Now, we're going to start again, and this time, you are going to listen to me. I. Will. Not. Turn. You. In. Did you get it that time?"

She struggled, but then he moaned—not as if he liked it or something, but in pain. It took her a moment to realize that she was the one that was hurting him. Shoving him off her, she looked at the mark on his shoulder. It was deep and would more than likely need stitches. But then she remembered that he was a shifter. He'd heal before she could get him to the hospital.

"I'm so sorry." Colton told her it was fine. "No, it's not fine, damn it. This is only a part of what I'm talking about. I can hurt you—I *did* hurt you. I haven't any idea what the fuck I can do. This stuff, all of it, is things that I neither asked for nor wanted. I have enough shit going on in my life that I don't need someone here that I could hurt accidently."

If he was going to say something, Colton was cut off by her dad getting in the rig. It wasn't like him to barge in without knocking. And when he turned to them, Dad then looked at her. He was pissed off.

"They're coming here." Her heart rate doubled, and she nearly fell down on the floor. "Your mother and Howard, they're on their way here. That was one of the messages that was on the machine. Howard said you were going to pay or he'd go to the papers again. He said that you would remember what happened the last time. Oh honey, what are you going to do?"

"What do they want?" Dad answered Colton's question by telling him that it was always the same, more money. "All right. I can deal with them if you want me to. Or you could just come to my house."

"No." She wanted this fucking day to end. "They'll hurt Dad if I'm not here. Howard and my mom will not only hurt my dad, but his business as well. Howard will trash the place and then tell people again. Dad has worked hard for his reputation, and they just don't care who they hurt when they think that they should have something."

"Blackmail." Even though it really wasn't a question, she nodded at Colton. "That's what you meant. They'll go to the newspaper about, I'm assuming, your nonexistent association with Nelson's. Is that the ten grand that your mother owes you?"

"No, that's on top of how much they've gotten from me over the years. I'd like nothing more than to tell them to fuck off, I no longer care. But I do." Colton nodded, but he didn't seem like he was paying attention to her anymore. Looking at her dad, she told him that he should go to the library or something. That she'd deal with them. "I don't want you here when they arrive. Okay?" He told her that it was a long drive and he'd be fine.

"I have a plan." Her dad was all for it, no matter what it

was. "You put something in the paper about how you were an inventor and that you inadvertently had one of your inventions sold off to an unscrupulous company. Tell them that you want to clear the air now, so that no one will think you've helped them in any way in what they did."

"How will that help, young man? And if you think this will keep them off her back, then I'm all for it." Colton grinned at her, and Hailey had a feeling that her mother and Howard were in for a rude awakening. But she couldn't do this to him. He had a reputation to uphold too. "Honey, if he has some connections that will keep them from hurting you and running you off again, I'm all for it."

"He's a doctor of good standing, Dad. If he helps and it doesn't work, or no one still believes me, then what do you think will happen to him?" Colton said that it mattered little to him. "You say that now. But what do you think is going to happen when you've run out of money, and the bill collectors and tax people are banging on your door for what you owe them?"

"I have an idea that you know that my family is wealthy, very much so." She nodded, and said that as a whole they more than likely were. "Yes, but we're also extremely wealthy as individuals. I have enough money and investments that if we lived to be two hundred years old, we'd never have to work again. And that would be counting taking care of your dad and anything that you want to pursue while you're not running off and trying to leave us both behind."

"Honey, I'm thinking that you should think about what he's saying. I love you dearly, but the thought of not having to work all the time, it sure does sound good. I know he was kidding, but I don't want to work all my life. I'm old. And you know as well as I do that Howard will never stop until they drain you dry. I can't see you suffering at their hands again." She told her dad that she'd take care of him. "I know you would, Hail, but what happens if neither of us have an income that'll put even a strawberry on the table between us?"

She was defeated. A few days ago she might have fought harder or even kicked them both out of her rig. But this was today, and she had no more fight left in her. Hailey was done fighting with everyone in her life.

"All right. I'll do what you want. Even be your mate if you still want it." Colton asked her if she was sure. "No, I'm not sure. But I've been left with no choice in the matter. I'd like you to leave my father's name out of this, if that's possible." She'd do anything in the world for her dad. He'd supported her. Even when she didn't live with him, Hailey could count on him to take her in and keep her safe. There was no way that she wasn't going to do the same for him. "I'll try, but when we're finished with whatever you want, I want my dad to be happy."

"He will be. He'll be able to sell his station and home for a great deal more than he owes on it." She told him that it was paid off. "Well good. When or if he wants to sell, he'll have a nice nest egg to fall back on. And we'll take care of him too."

Yes, she thought to herself, her father would be taken care of. He would have everything that he wanted. Not that she'd ever begrudge him anything. Her dad was everything to her. But what of her? Didn't anyone give a shit about what she wanted or needed? Oh well, she thought. At the very least, he'd be able to retire with a nice bit of cash if he sold the shop and house. And she would have a roof over her head, even though she didn't want it from Colton.

~*~

Colton drove them both to his house. He'd asked Dane what they could do about the paper, and she promised him that she would take care of it. That Hailey would almost be a hero when she was finished with her. After telling Hailey and her dad that, Peter had been excited, but Hailey had only thanked him. Like she just didn't care anymore.

Colton didn't know what to do with this Hailey. The other had been sassy and mouthy. She'd been brash and high-tempered. This version of her was something that he'd never seen on her since meeting her. And he was sure that her father hadn't either. He kept asking her if she was all right. And Peter got the same answer that Colton had gotten from her. "Yes, I'm fine."

He'd forgotten that Hailey had been to his house before, that she'd delivered at least three loads of furniture and things when he'd gotten the Spencer household. Some of the things were still needing to be set up, but the entire house was beautiful, elegant, and suited his tastes like he'd never thought that it would when he first started his expedition with his brothers.

"My goodness, Colton, this is a prime house. Must have put you back a couple of bucks." He told Peter that it really hadn't, he'd only needed to pay the back taxes. The expense had been in repairing what had been done to it while it sat there. "I used to do some work on houses, when I was younger and full of spit. This house, I'm telling you right now, is the most beautiful one I've seen in a long while."

"Then you'll positively love my brothers' homes. We all bought our homes to be closer to our parents." He pointed out where the other five brothers lived, and his mom and dad. But all the while, he was keeping an eye on Hailey.

"She's all right, I think. Just down about all this."

45

"I'm worried about her." Peter told him he was too when Hailey went around to the back of the house. "She seems so sad. Even with the two of us with her, she just seems like she's adrift and all alone."

"I'm sure that she'll come out of it. When her momma did to her what she did, that was what made her into what you saw the last few days. No prisoners, she told me. And she wasn't going to be a victim again, as she had been with them." Colton told Peter that he hadn't any idea what her mom had done. "Well, I'll tell you just a little, but I think that the rest of it should come from her. Her momma and that bastard Howard, they sold her off to a couple of men. I don't know much of what happened after that. I do know that they didn't hurt her, but she was never the same after that."

"There was nothing in the papers." Peter said that Hailey had escaped, he didn't know how, and was on the streets for a while. "So, no one reported it. They got away with whatever happened to her."

"Like I said, I don't know the details other than the little bit that she shared with me. But I do know that it changed her. For the better, I think really, but it still changed her." Colton knew for a fact that something like that would. He asked Peter how old she'd been. "Just before they kicked her out, right before she got out of college, so about thirteen or fourteen."

"She's smart then. Dane told me that she has a couple of PhDs to her name." Peter told him that it wasn't just that, not with her. "I don't understand. Do you mean her being able to create things?"

"No, she has one of those minds that can remember everything. And not just seeing but hearing and smelling stuff too. It's what made her take languages in college." They both looked in the direction she'd gone off to. "I can't tell you that I'm not worried about her. Especially when the Damons get here. And if they brought their brood with them...well, let's just not tell them that you've got money. I'd not bring them out here either."

"You think that they'll try and get some from me? That isn't going to happen, Peter. I protect what is mine, and my family. And as of the moment that I knew she was my mate, you both became a part of the family." Peter changed the subject then and asked to see the house. "I'd like for you both to stay here until they're gone. I can't be in two places at once, and I want to make sure that they don't hurt either of you."

"I'm all right at home. I am. They don't think I have a plug nickel. Thanks to Hailey, I can quit working, but it keeps me out of trouble and all." They entered the house and Peter whistled. "Holy Jehoshaphat. You struck it rich, didn't you, boy?"

Telling Peter how he'd come to have the furniture as he showed him around the house was fun. The man had a wonderful laugh that made him want to laugh with him. When they had gone through the entire upper floors, they headed into the living room.

"I still have things to purchase for this room. I didn't think that wooden benches and lawn chairs would blend well with the rest of the house. And there are a few things that I'd like to get for two of the bedrooms. What do you think?" Peter sat down on the couch that had been in the barn when he'd gotten his home. It was out of date, and he thought there was a spring or two that wanted to pinch if you sat too long. "Do you think this is something that Hailey would like too?"

"Oh, she'll love all the old furniture. She's got herself a bread cabinet that she's been working on for a while. Stripping it down to the wood and then cleaning it up. Her grandma thought that redecorating was to slap a coat of paint on everything and that was all it took. I think there might be as many coats on that thing as there are colors." Colton laughed and asked how long she'd been working on it. "Couple of years, I guess. She's not putting it off, but things have a habit of getting in the way when you're not looking."

"Yes, I have that happening to me all the time." When the door to the front of the house opened, he hoped it was Hailey and it was, thankfully. Having her in the room with them, Colton felt much better. She hadn't gotten over whatever was bothering her, but she did try, he could see. "I was just telling your dad here that I have a few more pieces to purchase for the house. Do you have any suggestions for this room?"

"Why would you ask me that?" He said that she was his mate, and he wanted her happy. When her laughter spilled from her lips, he felt his cat snarl at him. It was neither happy nor funny. She was really pissed off. "I have nothing to add to your home, Dr. Stanton. This is yours, not mine."

"Whatever I have is yours, Hailey. I'd like some input on it. And I'd like you to call me Colton, not Dr. Stanton." She didn't say anything but did turn her head. That was when he saw that she'd been crying. The tracks of her tears hurt him so much that he wanted to comfort her. Peter said he wanted to look around the yard and left them just as Hailey sat down on the couch her dad had just vacated. "Hailey, tell me what's wrong or I'm going to try and figure it out on my own. And don't tell me that you're fine. We both know that you're not."

"I have a lot on my mind. And I'd appreciate it if you just left me alone." She stood up and he waited while she paced the room. Whatever she was thinking about, it was hurting her inside. And thus, hurting him as well.

Colton tried to think what had happened that had changed her since they'd been to her house. It was then that realized that she was feeling like she'd lost. He wasn't sure what she'd lost just now, but it would come to him. Defeated was what she was feeling, he'd bet anything. Colton was a good doctor, and this had slipped by him.

"Would you and your father like to go to my parents' house for dinner? Mom said that you'd been there before." Hailey nodded. "Is that a yes that you've been there before, or a yes that you wouldn't mind going."

"My...my step family is coming here. I can't think beyond that right now." Colton asked her if she was afraid. "I am. I know them much better than any of you. And neither of them is going to go quietly in the night. That's not the way they get what they want."

"They're not going to get anything but their throats ripped out if they don't leave us alone." She touched her fingers to the books that he'd gotten and had only just put away. "Hailey, please talk to me."

"I'm not, but thanks." He asked her what that meant. "I'm not going to unload or burden you with any more of my problems. They're mine, just as much as this house is yours. I'm not going to ever call this home. Not because it's not beautiful and looks like every dream I've ever had of a house that I'd like to own. But the truth of the matter is, you got what you wanted because I'm in trouble. I feel no less like a whore than when my mother sold me to men to rape me for money. So, if you don't mind, don't try analyzing me. I'm doing what you want."

When she left him there, he was too shocked to go after her. Colton had a feeling that she'd not leave here—she'd told him that she would stay. But her reactions to him trying to help her were way off the line. He started to stand up to shake some sense into her when he heard from Dane that there was a fire at Hailey's home, and she wondered if Hailey or her father were at home.

No, her and her father are with me at our house. He went to the front door and yelled for Peter. Hailey came from the kitchen. "Someone has set fire to your home, I think."

Chapter 4

It was a total loss, only one wall stood. The fire department was now only trying to keep it from burning the surrounding houses. Even Dad's working area, the garage at the side that he'd built with Pete, was engulfed in hot flames. Her project with her dad was gone as well.

"At least we weren't home." She nodded to her dad but said nothing. There were so many things in there that she would never be able to replace. Then it occurred to her that meant her grandma's cabinet and the pretty hankies that she'd given her were gone as well. Everything, her past life, was simply gone. "Honey, it'll be all right. We have insurance, and I'll just get me something closer to town. Maybe I can find something closer to you and Colton."

Her rig was the first thing that she'd moved when she got here. It was now back far enough from the fire that it hadn't been harmed. It was the only thing that had been saved. She watched as a wall from where her room had been fell over into the basement, along with whatever had been in there. She just

51

couldn't help it—Hailey cried harder.

Big arms went around her, and she felt a warm hard chest beneath her cheek. Hailey knew that it could only be one person, but right now, she was hurting in ways that he'd never understand or care to. Colton was just there, that was all. She wasn't leaning on him for support.

When she had cried herself out, she pulled away from him and stared at the fire. Just one more peg in her fucking shitty day. Not only had she lost everything that they had, but she would have to live with Colton until her dad bought another house.

"Are you all right?" She smiled at Lucy and told her what she'd said to everyone who had asked. She was fine. "They're just things, Hailey. Things that you can replace. But you and your father are safe, and that's the best thing."

Nodding at her, Hailey told her again that she was all right. And when she hugged her tightly, Hailey used all she had left not to cry again. That shit got you nothing but more heartache.

Her dad came to talk to her several times as she stood there, as did the rest of Colton's family. He didn't leave her side, but she knew better than to depend on him to make things better. Simply put, she was at his mercy.

After the fire department finished up and there were only a few places that were still smoldering, the chief came to talk to her and her father. She had no idea if Colton was with them or not. Hailey was numb. She didn't think that she could have one more thing piled on her.

"This is just a guess, but I do believe it was arson." Dad asked if it could have been anything to do with the things he had in the garage. "No, sir. The fire started at the back of the house—gas cans were found back there. Then cinders bounced

52

to the garage and burned there too. When we first were called, it was the house that was burnt the most; the garage started later."

She asked him what they did now. "We have insurance and it's up to date." He told her that she'd be responsible for contacting the company and they'd ask for a report. "All right. We'll take care of that first thing in the morning. Thank you."

"Do you and your dad have a place to go, Hail? I mean, there is nothing left here." Colton said that they were going to be staying with him. "That's good news. The Stantons, you couldn't do better than them to have helping you. If you need anything, you just give me a call. And if you think of someone that might have had a grudge against you, that would be helpful too."

"My ex-wife and her new husband." Chief Anderson asked if they were in town. "I don't know if they're actually in town, but they'd be close by now, I guess. From what I'm to understand, they had left their home a couple of hours ago. Come to think of it, I forgot—it's been a messy sort of day. Milly down at the hardware store talked to them. She said they were fit to be tied about us not being home. We were looking at Colton's home when we heard about this."

Hailey walked away from them and ended up by her rig. She sat on the back end of it, just to have a place to sit down, when Colton joined her again. There were just too many reasons for her not to have to have a civil conversation with him right now.

"I have nothing to say to you. Please, I've had a really shitty day, and this is just the icing on the top. So, I'd ask you if I could just be left alone." He said that he wanted to talk to her about what she'd said at his house. "Not now, damn it. Everything

I owned was in there. My car, my grandma's cabinet. My diplomas and all the things that I collected while in college. I have nothing at all. And if you don't fucking mind, I need time to deal with this."

He stood there for several seconds. She saw his cat move along his arms, and wondered if he was going to come out and devour her. It wouldn't have surprised her at all if he did. At this point, Hailey might welcome death over what she'd been told and had been done to her in the last twelve hours. When he walked away, his back stiff, she turned from the fire and looked at the dense trees behind her dad's house.

"I've come to talk to you." She told Denny that she was talked out today. "Then you can listen to me. We're trying our best to make you welcome and happy, but you keep right on pushing us away at every turn. Now, I know that you're hurting, and I can understand what you might be going—"

"Are you telling me that I should be grateful that the wonderful and rich Stantons have come to help me? Or that someone in the family made me into something I don't understand, nor did I want it?" She laughed bitterly. "Since I've met your family, everything and anything that I had is now gone."

"You can't be blaming that on us. We didn't do anything to make this happen to you. And I'm sorry that Dane tried to help you out and turned you into whatever you are right now. But she was only thinking of you and what this might have done to you." He stood up straighter, his anger almost something that she could touch. And for some reason, Hailey thought that this man never got angry with anyone. "Colton is trying his best to make things easier for you but you continue to push him away. What burr do you have up your butt that you'd scoff at everything that we're trying to do for you?"

She looked at Denny, a really nice man, and thought about what he'd said to her. Hailey knew that Colton hadn't sent him here, and more than likely had said nothing to any of them. But his dad was here because she'd hurt his son. Looking to the trees again, Hailey knew that fighting was futile. She was done.

"I'm not pushing him away anymore. He can do whatever he wants. Also, I won't do anything to your family again. I'm sorry, Dr. Stanton." He didn't say anything—Hailey thought he looked as if he didn't understand her. "I'll tell Dr. Stanton, your son, that I'm sorry too. I'm done."

She went to find Colton to tell him, too, that she was sorry. When she found him, he was with his other brothers and their wives. Asking if she could speak to him for a moment, he peeled away from the others and she told him she was sorry.

"You don't have to be sorry, Hailey. I just want to help you. And to clear the air about what you said to me at the house." She nodded. "I don't understand what it is you think that I've won. You're my mate and I'm yours. I want to make sure that you're safe and that nothing more happens to you."

"Yes, I understand that." Her heart was crumbling, and she had to swallow three times before she could continue. "I understand that you're trying to help, and I was getting in your way. I won't again."

~*~

He wanted to pick her up and hold her. Also, to bend her over his knee and beat her ass. And he was holding on to his temper, which wasn't making his cat any better either. He told her again that he wanted to know what she was talking about. When she looked at him, the anger there was evident, and he could almost feel the heat of it.

"I've asked you and your family several times to leave me alone. To let me be and I'd be all right. Do you have any idea what I've gone through the past few days? I killed a man, and nearly died. Then I woke up in a stranger's home." He told her that he knew that. "Yeah? Well, you don't know the half of it, you asshole. I woke up a stranger to my own body. I've had my house burnt to the ground, with not only everything that I owned, but everything that I held near to my heart in it. It's all gone. I can dress myself, and I can change my hands into lethal weapons. And on top of all that, I have a fucking pushy mate that won't give me five fucking minutes to deal with this. Even your father has come and told me how ungrateful I am being, because the king of the castle, his son, is my mate and I should be ever so grateful to him." He started to speak. "So, if you ask me, you have won. I have nothing left. No emotions, no memories. Hell, I don't even have my own body back, because the Stantons knew better than anyone how I should be."

When she turned and walked away from him, this time he let her. Colton could hear her crying as she made her way to the other side of the street and continued walking. He had been pushy, and so had his family. And while he didn't think his dad had said those things to her exactly, he had a feeling that it would have come across like that when she'd been hurting.

His dad came to ask him where Hailey had gone. "I've upset her. And I've angered her. I have a feeling that it's not going to change much until she thinks this through on her own. I've really fucked up." Dad said that he might have gotten a little mouthy with her too. "Yes, she told me. And we all need to leave her alone. At least for now. She's hurting." He told his dad the list of things that she'd dealt with, including what Dad had said to her.

"I never thought of it like that. I mean, all I could see was that she was hurting you and there was no reason for it." Colton watched her go into the restaurant that was on the main drag into town. "I need to tell her I'm sorry. I never meant to make her day even worse."

"I don't think any of us did. But I screwed up with her as badly as the others. Hell, it was worse than they treated their mates when they came here. I hurt her emotionally, and like you, could only see that she was hurting me." Dad asked him what he was going to do about it. "To be honest, I haven't any idea. Be there for her, but not talk to her about moving in, protecting her, or how what she's doing is affecting me. I need to consider all the shit that has happened to her since she became a member of the family, and let her deal with it."

"All right, son. You tell us what you need for us to do, and we'll hold off on talking to her too."

Colton nodded and thought about the day that he'd had with her. Instead of treating her like she might be overwhelmed, when he could see that she was for himself, he'd in effect pushed her further and further away.

"You'd think that I'd know better. I should have stepped back, listened to her when she spoke instead of wanting to fix everything." He looked at his dad, his hero. "I'm a dumbass. I hurt her — inadvertently, yes, but I did hurt her."

"Yes. When I think of the things that I said to her, I wasn't a nice man. I was angry at her for making you — what I thought was — jump through hoops when she should have been in awe of you." Colton laughed when his father did. "What's the plan, Colton? I'm here for you."

"I don't know just now, but I need some dinner. I think that her dad and I will go there, have a nice dinner, and ask her what she'd like to do from now on. I should have been doing that all along, but she's a very resourceful woman and can and probably has taken care of things all her life. I just got in the way."

Peter said that he could eat again. The house was pretty much done burning out, and he knew that someone from the fire department would be there all evening with it, just in case. Walking to the restaurant, he told Peter what he'd just told his own father.

"She is very independent. And all kinds of stubborn. I told you she wasn't like this when she was younger. Hail would do whatever anyone wanted of her, and not care one whit how it might affect her plans. But then her mother and Howard, they messed things up, and she got herself a backbone harder and straighter than anything you'd ever see." Peter looked at him. "Well, I guess you might have seen a bit of it, but she's— Holy crap, they're in there with her."

He looked in the diner and saw Hailey standing up toe to toe with a big man, who was almost as round as he was tall. Since he'd never met any of them, he figured that the kids were theirs, as well as that the woman right behind the man was Hailey's mom.

Instead of going in with both guns blazing, Colton went to the back door and slipped into the place without disturbing any of what was going on. It was time for him to let her wear the pants in their relationship and he'd put them on when she needed him. This might be the hardest thing he'd ever set before himself.

Chapter 5

Howard hated Hailey — he had since she'd first come to live with them when she'd been no more than about two or three. Christ, she was a pain in the ass, and he'd never forgiven her for escaping from their plan to get rid of her since he'd had to pay the men back. Fucking bitch would never be reliable, nor would she do what he had wanted. He was her fucking stepfather, for fuck's sake, and she'd better start listening to him.

He noticed the man behind her, but he wasn't worried. Hailey was a loner, someone that fought her own battles. She'd never want a man like that one in her life simply because he might hit her. Howard wished that he had hit her more when she'd been living with them.

The man was big with a slim build but muscled too. Howard found himself hating him too, simply because of his looks. Holding in his stomach as best he could, Howard nearly passed out after only a few seconds of trying to hide his fat.

"Just fucking do what you're told, or so help me, Hailey, you are going to regret it. What do you think your sperm donor

59

will do if you take away his only income? Give over the cash, and we'll hold off on going to the papers again." Howard saw sperm donor sitting in a booth behind Hailey. "Did you call your daddy dear to come and help you out of this? There is no way you can be helped, Hailey. You fucked up, and you're going to pay me to keep quiet about it."

When he looked at the man again, Howard was sure that he wasn't with Hailey. First of all was the size thing. Then there was the fact that he just smelled of money and breeding. Howard thought, but only for a second or two, that he'd find out what he wanted. But honestly, he just didn't care so long as she forked over some cash for him. Hailey turned and looked at the man behind her.

"I have this. What are you doing here?" The man told Hailey that he knew that she was capable of handling this, he was only here for moral support. "Yeah? Who the hell are you, and what did you do with the real Stanton?"

When she turned to Howard once more, he drew back to hit her. The low growl startled him a bit, but the man, if it had been him that growled, only smiled. Hitting Hailey gave him so much pleasure, especially when he was able to knock her on her ass. Linda told him to hit her and take whatever she had on her.

"I wouldn't if I were you." He laughed at Hailey and asked her what she was going to do about it. "Kill you."

It was said so calmly that Howard had a moment of fear. She just stared at him until he heard something hard hit the table next to them. She had a gun there, and her hand was still on it. Howard wasn't stupid enough that he thought he could outrun a bullet, so he put his fist down.

"This isn't over, bitch." Hailey shrugged, another thing that she did that really pissed him off. Like she didn't care. "You have twenty-four hours to come up with the cash, or something else you find so dear to your heart will go up in flames."

"You set fire to my dad's house." It wasn't a question, but he didn't fall for that old trick. There wasn't any way that he was going to admit to anything. "You'll be happy to know that both of us have a better place to stay. And should you even attempt to go there, if one fucking foot of your body touches that land, and I will turn the wolves on you. You know I will, Howard. I've done it before."

"You fucking cunt." Linda moved him out of the way and slapped Hailey across the face. And when she hit her mother back, he was as surprised as the man behind Hailey. "You fucking bitch, you hit me."

"You hit me too. A great many more times than I've had the pleasure of hitting you. Now, take your brats before they tear up the rest of this place, and get the fuck out of here. There will be no money, not again, even if you gave me ten years to gather it up for you. And as far as the paper, you go right on ahead with it. You'll find that no one cares about it as much as you do."

"Yeah? You're wrong about that, Hailey. I think the information coming from your mom will carry a lot of weight. And once I tell them how abusive you've been to me all my life, who do you think is going to win then?" Linda laughed and Howard joined her. Yes, this was getting better now. "You are going to give us money, and you'll do it before we are ready to leave."

They both left, going out the door after telling the kids to come along. He'd given them each a knife when he'd seen Hailey sitting at a table with another woman. While he'd been making sure that Hailey knew who was in charge, he'd told the kids to cut the place up. She'd have to pay for that as well.

"You think that man was with her?" He asked Linda if he looked like he was. "I don't know, Howie. If she has a man in her corner, especially one like that one, we might have to threaten her long distance again. And did you see the way that Peter just sat there, acting like he didn't care that we were taking care of his daughter? Moron. What a fucking moron he is."

"The man behind her isn't any of our concern. Do you think that he'd let her be slapped and screamed at if he was anything to her? No, he'd be shoving her out of the way and taking over, as I would do for you. Men are so much stronger, and have a better hold on their temper. No, he wasn't with her." Howard knew that he was right. "But the next time we talk to her, we'll get her all alone. And I need to get me a gun too. That way if she pulls hers again, we'll be able to have one too."

He had no idea how to go about getting a gun, or even how to fire one. He'd seen the newspaper that said that she was a hero and had a registered gun. He and Linda had thought this would be a perfect time to threaten her again, while people were still thinking that she was something special.

They drove back to the little hotel on Route Forty and told the kids to fucking shut up. He had to think.

"Okay, you have that article all ready to go, right? I mean, once she pays us, I want to make sure that it hits the paper as soon as we can put it there." This was going to be epic, he thought. They'd get money, and he'd be able to shame her again so that she'd had to leave the little town she was staying in. And an added bonus was that Peter would be ruined as well. Win-win for them.

"Yes, I even have pictures of me from that time that I had

the car accident. You remember, they had a fit at the hospital that I'd been driving so fast and me carrying. All it did was manage to bruise my body up. I'm going to say that she beats me on a regular basis—what do you think?" He told her that he loved it. Anything to get her into trouble. "Oh, I even put in here how she never has anything to do with her other siblings, and that should make people know what sort of person they're calling a hero."

"I want her to pay for every little thing that she's cost us. And make up for the fact that we get no more food stamp cards, or even a little cash from the government fucks in order to pay the heat bill." He thought of that day they'd been there to get their cash to pay off bills, and how they'd been arrested instead. Nor would any bank or even a loan shark lend them enough money to pay for a paper, much less go out to dinner or have a good vacation. "She's a fucking bitch. And I cannot believe that you and she are from the same gene pool."

There were things that let someone know that they were related. The red hair was one thing, and the porcelain-like skin color too. Of course, now Linda's was more gray than red, and she'd been going to tanning booths since he'd known her and her freckles no longer looked like anything but old age spots. But she loved him and he her, so that didn't matter so much.

"Once we have her where we want her, I think we should outright tell her that she's on a payment plan now. That she will have to pay us monthly for keeping quiet." He told his wife that they weren't going to be able to hold that over her head if they put it out there first. "Oh, but we will. We'll have her sign a contract. Something that says that she has to pay us no matter what. I even looked up an attorney to have him make sure that it's all right."

"That is brilliant, my dear, simply brilliant." And it was, too. He and Linda together, they could come up with ways to scam people better than anyone he knew. Sometimes they'd do it for some cash, but other times, they just did it to sort of keep in practice. "You have a very devious mind, Linda. I love you for it."

He decided that he needed to make a list of things that he wanted in the contract that they were going to have put together. Howard hadn't any idea how they were going to pay for that, but they'd figure out something before they were finished with it. A contract. He'd never have thought of that, not in a million years, he thought.

There wasn't a pool at the hotel they were in. They'd gone for cheap rather than nice. While they both had a little cash and pooled it together, they didn't have things like money to go out to eat and such. So, until they got money from Hailey, they'd brought them a hot plate and a bunch of meals they could heat up to save their funds. After this, they had promised their kids that they'd go to one of them big parks and stay a week for them all.

He worked on his list for the better part of the day. The air conditioning made the room only slightly tolerable, but it was better than nothing, he supposed. A pool would have been nice, but he knew that would have cost more money. So, with his kids screaming at each other and his wife screaming at them, he made his way to the bathroom to think. It was the only place that he could think to go that had a lock on the door.

Howard had another list too. This one told how much money they needed to really pay everything off this time, and what he'd do with the leftovers. Of course, there wasn't as much left over as he thought there should be, simply because they really were in over their heads with credit cards and just regular bills. So while he was thinking of what he was going to get from Hailey, he marked off things that he thought could slide until the next bunch of cash came in from her.

There wasn't any reason for him not to have a job, other than the fact that he didn't want to work. He could have his pick of a hundred jobs in their little town, but he thought it was too much effort to even go someplace and apply. Then there was the fact that he'd have to be at a job all day, and would be, he supposed, expected to work. In a word, Howard was lazy.

When he did have a job, Howard would work harder at not working, or at least giving the illusion that he was, than he did the actual work that they'd hired him for. He lost every job that he'd had, going from just being a burger flipper to working in hot dirty warehouses. Then they'd hit on the idea that they were going to be rich on someone else's dime. That just happened to be Hailey.

Laughing to himself, he thought of the first time she'd given them cash. He had a list then, of paying off all their bills to be caught up. But he wanted to celebrate with his kids that they were going to be better off. Then there was the big screen television that was on sale. After that, there wasn't enough to pay off everything, so he just said fuck it and spent the money on all kinds of things that they'd had to do without while not working.

He looked down at his list and added a motor home to it. One of the kind that you could drive around like a big bus and not have to worry about kids in the back seat whining about how they were bored out of their minds. He wanted to put them out of his mind, but Linda loved them, and he couldn't get rid of them because of that. Selling them off would have been a good money maker.

Howard thought about the cash that they'd gotten by putting an ad in the newspaper about selling off their prime daughter. Hailey had developed earlier than most kids her age, and looked the part of a teenager back then. He had two buyers for her, and they each had to pay ten grand to have her, and an extra ten grand to the one of them that wanted to take her first. There had been a bidding war over her, and they'd ended up with nearly fifty grand, on top of the twenty the men had paid to have her.

Then she'd fucked that up by escaping from them. Howard thought the men he'd sold her to might have had something to do with that, but he never got the chance to ask. They were going to take him to court and have him put in jail. While he didn't know how that was going to work, he knew that they'd make it stick. They were old fuckers, he'd found out, but they were also lawyers that could make it work out for them.

Coming out of the bathroom when the kids were pounding on the door to be let in to use it, he laid down on the bed and closed his eyes. The thoughts that were circling his head spun too fast for him to think about, but the dollar signs there were making him excited to get this ball rolling. Yes, sir, they would make a killing off of this shit. And Hailey would be ruined, right along with her fucking dad.

He knew that he should be helping Linda with the kids — they certainly had become a handful — but he was exhausted from figuring out the plan, and knew that she'd not begrudge him getting some rest.

~*~

Hailey was shaking so badly when her mother and Howard left that had it not been for Colton standing behind her to catch

66

her, she would have fallen. He took her to the booth with her dad and laid her head down on the table.

"I didn't need you to stand behind me." Colton told her that he knew that. "Then why were you? I'm sure they thought that you were going to rescue me from whatever they said to me. Well, I've got news for you, I've heard that before, and am quite capable of taking care of them myself."

"I know that as well. As for standing behind you, I was making sure that you didn't hurt them. I have to tell you, Hailey, when you hit your mom back, I could have jumped to the moon, I was so happy." Hailey didn't know what to think of this version of Colton. It was as if he was now someone that supported her as an equal, not as a dumbass. "Your dad and I came here for some dinner. He said that he has to watch his carbs, and I told him that was a good idea. Would you like to join us?"

She told him that apparently, she was. He only grinned at her. The man was going to drive her to drink, she swore. When the waitress came to take their order, she told her right away that her and her dad were on one check and that Dr. Stanton was all by himself. Instead of telling her that he had it, he only nodded. Then he asked to speak to May if she was around.

When the big woman came out from the back of the restaurant, she hugged Colton tightly in her ample arms. She told him that she was glad he'd been there; those people might have been coming to her domain to make a mess there too.

"I want to pay for all this damage. All right?" She said that it would certainly put a hole in her budget to have to replace all this stuff. It wasn't until then that Hailey realized what had gone on when she'd been arguing. "And if you see your way into changing out that bench that gets you all the time, I'd surely pay for that too. I have ruined many a pants on that sucker."

May was still laughing about it as she wobbled her way to the back room. There was something going on here, and Hailey wasn't sure what it was. Nor did she understand Colton. What happened to Bossy McBossy? Why didn't Colton take over, shoving her out of the way as soon as he got there? She looked at him as her dad's salad was set in front of him.

"What's wrong with you? And why didn't you tell me to go home like a good little girl?" Colton asked her if she would have. "No. They're my relatives, not yours."

"That's right. And the simple fact is, I didn't need to take over. You had it well under control." She played with the condensation on her glass while he continued. "I'm sorry about before. All of it. I treated you horribly, and I'm sorry."

Hailey was no less confused when her burger was brought to her, along with a huge plate of fries. It was a downfall of hers, fries. She didn't eat them with catsup like most people did, but loved barbecue sauce to dip them in. She had a few fries and looked at him again. There was some sort of something going on, and she didn't like that he wasn't like he'd been all day.

"What are you playing at? Are you trying to butter me up for sex? I won't, no matter what you say or do." Her dad told her to behave, and she felt her face heat up. But she looked at Colton again and he was smiling at her. A friendly smile that warmed her up. "Well?"

"No, I'm not trying to butter you up. Though the thought of sex with you is appealing. But I'm trying to make up for what I've been doing all day. And my family. We've been pushing and pushing you into a corner, and it was only recently pointed out to me that I'm an ass and treating you no differently than my brothers did their wives when they joined the family."

Hailey asked him who happened to be smarter than him. "Me. I really didn't mean anything by it, only to keep you safe. I've decided that I need to back off and let you deal with things that make you feel better, because we're both aware I don't know your family or what they might do as well as you would. And again, I'm sorry for that."

"Your dad got to you? Or someone?" He said that his dad now felt badly for what he'd said to her too. "Yeah, well, I'll believe that when I see it. He was right in some things—I am pushing you away. But you pushed harder. I told you I only needed a fucking minute, and you didn't seem to get that."

"I do now."

He bit into his burger, and she could smell the bacon he had on his. Hailey asked her dad if his dinner was all right, and he said that he'd rather have a burger and fries, but he was all right. Colton finished his burger and part of hers when she offered it to him. The fries were only hers, however.

When they were asked if they wanted pie, she declined. She wasn't much of a dessert person, only having the sweet treat on occasion. While she did enjoy a big bowl of fresh mixed fruit, pies and cakes were not a part of that.

Colton ate his cherry pie with ice cream, and her and dad sat there with him. She supposed that she could have left them there, gone someplace that didn't have Colton there, but she was enjoying the company of her dad.

"I was wondering something. Your stepfather, he mentioned that you were going to be in trouble with the paper, but you seemed to not care. Why? Or are you anticipating the article that will come out in the morning?" She said that Dane and Tess had come to talk to her before her parents got there. "That makes sense. Whatever she has written, is that something

69

that you liked?"

"She only told me the highlights. But she did warn me of a few things with the Damons." She looked at her dad and saw him give her a little nod. Hailey glanced around the room and saw for the most part they were alone. "My mother, her and Howard tried to sell me off to a group of men. I had been drugged and tied up in this hotel room about ten minutes from their home. They...I was beaten before anyone arrived, and it weakened me to the point that I'd not be able to fight them off me."

"They deserve to die—you know that, don't you?" She nodded and looked at her dad when he asked if he could go on to the house, to Colton's house. "Yes, you go on ahead, Peter. My staff there, they're expecting you. They have a couple of rooms ready for you and your daughter."

"I'm not going to sleep with you. I don't care if I have to sleep on the street, I'm not going to do that for a place to live." He nodded and said that he'd had her a room, her own room, set up too. "You don't want to sleep with me?"

Instead of answering her, he pulled her to him by cupping the back of her head and kissed her. Kissed her made it sound as if their lips touched and that was all. But this was consuming, heated in a way that she'd never felt before with any man. And when he let her go and went to the other side of the table, across from her, she could see the outline of his cock against his jeans.

Hailey didn't know what to say, so she sat there trying to get her thought process back under control. When he said her name, she looked up at him and felt her anger surge forward. But before she could unleash it on him, he asked her to wait just a moment before she tore his head off.

"I do want you. And as I said before, you know what our

kind is like, so you know that being around you isn't easy without wanting you. But, and this is a promise I am going to keep for you, I will take nothing from you unless you allow it. Kissing you just then, it was that or throw you up on this table and have a feast of your body." Hailey nodded. For some reason she knew that he was telling her the truth. "Now, I'd like to know as much as I can about the other couple. He mentioned some things that I'm sure make better sense to you. So if you could, just so I'm aware of them in all ways, what else did they do to you?"

They had been cruel to her, even before Howard moved in with them. Her mother had been different too. Not that she had ever been mean or anything like that—she'd been indifferent to her. But after Howard, it got to be that she could do nothing right.

"I won a scholarship, a full ride to the state college. I would have to live on campus the first year, but they made arrangements for me to have a house with a family rather than a dorm with lots of people much older than I was." He asked her what she'd studied. "At first I wanted to become a linguist. Work in the United Nations building to help translate when people came in. But I had to take an elective, and that introduced me to gears and electricity, and how the two of them could be put together to make something that others would benefit from."

"Dane mentioned that you had all kinds of things that you worked on or perfected." Hailey told him that she'd found a way to make a simple hydraulic on a shopping cart—it had been simple and the first of her designs. "I've never seen them. Are they used anywhere around here?"

"No, the production on them was all set to work when they realized that the cost of the carts rebuilt like that would be cost

71

prohibitive. Especially since they were going to let people use them for free. They wanted to make money off them rather than help their fellow man." He said that he'd run into that as well. "That was the first of my things, and it paved the way for me to stay at school and get my PhD on a couple of other things as well. But, you might think that I was cheating on the language doctorial. I have a total recall of everything that I encounter. Or an eidetic memory."

"Your dad mentioned that. He said that's why you could do so well in college." She said that it had certainly helped a great deal. "What else can you tell me about you? I mean, I'm assuming that you had a shitty childhood, what with your parents splitting up."

"Actually, them getting a divorce was the best thing that the two of them could have done. At the time, Dad told me that he'd had no idea that my mother was not only sleeping around, but she was also stealing from the place where she worked. As well as taking Dad's money that was supposed to be going into a pension for him. I think that's mostly why he works. He's afraid of not having anything to fall back on when he gets older." She told him about what she'd done to help him out with that too. "The house had been paid off and all the taxes were caught up. I have no way of adding to his pension without causing him trouble, so I just helped him out with bills and such after that. Paying off his home was the least I could do for him."

"Those men, the ones that you were sold to, did anything ever become of them?" Hailey told him that she couldn't prove anything, and they weren't talking. "I can see that. But it must have been hard for you to go back to them after that."

"I didn't. When I was home that time, the time that it happened, I was only a few weeks short of graduating. I wasn't in very good shape after that, but I managed to make it to exams and such to get out." Hailey wondered why it had been so easy to tell him this, but continued. "My arm was broken, as well as my left ankle, when my parents tied me up. I also had a concussion, as well as bruising around my ribs where they'd kicked me there. The men, I think they were more appalled about what they'd paid for than anything. And they cut the chains off me and left me there. It was another two days before I could move enough to call for my dad."

"You have not had a good life. And I didn't help by adding more to it, did I?" She didn't say anything, but thought of how everyone assumed that they knew what was better for her than she did. "Why don't we head home and relax watching television? I will have to hook it up. I've not decided where it's to go yet, but we can work on that too."

"All right." She sat there for a minute longer, neither of them moving. "I don't want to be your mate, Colton. I'm sorry about that. But I don't need anyone else making decisions for me and keeping me what they think is in line."

"Yes, I can understand that. I truly can. But I'm going to change. I never meant to do any of those things to you." She didn't know if she should believe him or not, so didn't say anything. "Oh, before I forget, the Fourth of July is in a week. And Mom and Dad have this big bash. I hope you will go with me."

Chapter 6

Colton was called away in the middle of the night. Driving to the police station, he thought about how nice it was to have someone to share a night with. Not that he'd been dying for dates, but he liked knowing that she was going to be around for the rest of his life. If, and this was a big if, he could maintain himself.

He and Hailey had gone up to bed at the same time. Colton knew that she was expecting him to go back on his word, to make her come to his room. It had been hard, yes, but when she went into her room and he walked down to his, he actually felt better about this than he had before.

The drive wasn't that long, and he made it to the station in good time. Going into the station house, he asked what he was working with. The arresting officer told him that the man had claimed that Jesus told him that he needed to murder his entire family because they weren't human. Neither was he, but he decided to keep that bit of information to himself.

"Who are you?" He told the man that was chained to the

table his name. "They told me that someone was coming here to see me. I really don't need anyone around. I did what the Lord told me to do, and that shouldn't be any reason for me to be arrested."

"Why is that? I mean, you murdered your wife, her mother and yours, along with two of your three children. I do think that is reason enough. Unless, of course, you can convince me otherwise." The man didn't look as if he was going to answer him, so Colton spoke again. "Do you really think that the Lord would have you murder a four-year-old, as well as an infant? What could they have done to warrant such behavior from him."

"You should tell them to let me go. I've done nothing wrong at all." Not an answer, but he really hadn't expected one.

He looked down at the file that he'd been handed before coming in here. The children had been shot once in the back of the head. The others had been beaten first, then strangled enough to put bruising on their necks before he shot them in the head. Facing them this time.

"What do you suppose is going to happen to your daughter now, the one that wasn't home? I mean, you spared her. What are you going to do about that since she is still alive?" Colton opened the file up and read over the report. "It says here that she is six years old and staying with her aunt. Did you send her there, or did she escape your murdering spree?"

"She's all right because I wasn't to kill her. Billy is my darling." That sent all kinds of alarms going off in Colton's head, and he asked the man what made her so special. "She's my darling. I wasn't to kill her. She's special."

Colton reached out to his friend and cop that worked in this department. He'd gotten to know all the people working there over the years, and he asked him to have Billy examined by the doctor again. This time he asked that she be checked for sexual abuse.

I just got the report back now. Hang on and let me read it over. She didn't say anything when we went to pick her up. Not like a little girl should have, seeing all the police around. He asked Drew to hurry. *Holy shit! She's not only been sexually abused, Colton, but they swabbed her mouth and found semen. Christ, what the fuck is this world coming to?*

Did they get any DNA from it? Drew told him that it would take a few days. *I have an idea that he says she's special because he's abused her. And perhaps his family found out about it. I want you to call my brother's wife and ask Dane if she can hurry this along for me. Tell her what we think has happened here.*

All right. This wouldn't happen to be the scary one, would it? Christ, she comes around and nearly all my men are ready to confess to shit they had nothing to do with. Even shit that happened before they were born, I'm betting. But I'll call her. Just be warned, the station house is going to be in an uproar when she shows up. Colton warned him that all his sisters were scary, and that he'd take the responsibility if that indeed happened. *Thanks. Calling her now.*

He continued to talk to the man. His name wasn't important to him, and Colton had found it easier to talk to someone that might be having mental issues that he didn't know. He didn't ask this man's name, and it wasn't on the file either. Just the way he liked it.

"I was going to ask you how she was special. But I think I know, don't I?" The man looked at him sharply and asked him what he thought he knew. "Well, she's six years old. What do you think I meant?"

"You don't know what you're talking about. You just mind your own business like I want you to." Colton nodded, and the man seemed to calm down again. "I'm a good daddy to her."

"I'm sure that you are. But your family, they didn't think so, did they?" He was agitated again—this time Colton could see him clenching and unclenching his fists. "Is that why you murdered them? They didn't like that your daughter was special?"

"You stay away from her, you hear me? They wanted to take her away, and I told them she was special." He felt the first touch of someone trying to reach him. It had been about an hour, so he knew it was going to be Dane. But it was Hailey instead.

I can't talk to you right now, honey. I'm working. She said that was fine, when he had time then.

He looked at the man in front of him again—he was getting madder by the minute. The he heard from Dane. *You did it all ready? Christ, that was fast.*

Colton, I want you to listen to me carefully and not freak the fuck out. Colton told her that was causing the exact reaction that she'd told him not to have. *Hailey and her father are with Brayden and me. They're both fine, but they've been in an accident. Someone sideswiped their car and ran them off the road. We're at the hospital with them. And they're both all right. Her dad has a few cuts, and Hailey has healed from whatever happened to her.*

But they're both all right? Dane promised him that they were. *She reached out to me a few minutes ago. I told her I was working. I wish she would have told me what was going on.*

She's still really shook up. I don't think it was so much the accident as it was her healing herself. I've yet to find out what she was healed from, but I'll have it sooner or later. After asking again and being assured that they were fine, Colton told Dane that he'd sent her a sample of DNA. *Yes, I've got it. We're at the hospital, but let me get in touch with someone there. They can read whatever came back on the machine.*

He was too shook up himself to talk to the man anymore. Instead, he just let him prattle on about how his daughter was very special to him. That she wasn't going to be taken from him because the Lord had told him to kill the others so that they'd not harm her. So when Dane came back with a positive marker that it was her father's semen, and that he was already in the system for sexual misconduct, she said it had been easy. And there was a restraining order against him with the wife and children.

"I believe that you killed them because they had taken Billy away from you, didn't you?" He told him to shut his mouth. "No, I don't think so. You no more heard from the Lord than anyone else did. I believe that you killed them all, your ex-wife, your mother-in-law, as well as your own mom. Plus, your two children. You aren't insane, you're sick."

The man leapt at him, and Colton was able to dodge out of his reach before he could touch him. The table had also hindered him from hurting Colton. When the police came in and took him away, Colton gathered up his paperwork to go to the hospital. He would write the report later.

It seemed to take forever to get to the ER. Colton set his cruise control so that he'd not speed. It was difficult to manage because all he wanted to do was hold Hailey, but he made it there in one piece and made his way to the emergency room to find her.

Colton found Peter first. He was banged up pretty badly, but nothing was broken. Colton asked him what had happened,

79

all the while wanting to find Hailey, when Peter laughed.

"Go see her. And I expect you to come back here and give me details too. She's about three rooms down from here."

Shaking his hand, Colton took off to the hall again. He was just ready to scream for her when Brayden came into the hall from one of the little rooms.

"Don't go in there yet." He asked his brother why not. "Because you look like a mad man. Your hair is all mussy. You're shaking, and I've never heard you talk so fast. Just take a deep breath, let it out, and try to calm yourself. Also, your cat is showing. You'll scare her if you go in there like this."

Colton nodded. Brayden was very calm, so he knew that Hailey would be all right. When he felt like he had some control over his beast and his mind, he asked how he looked now. Brayden moved so that he could enter the room she was in.

She'd been crying, he could see that. And when he asked her how she was doing, she reached for him, sobbing, and he held her. Colton was vaguely aware that Dane had left them. He lifted Hailey's chin up when she started to slow in her sobbing.

"Are you all right? I mean, you look all right to me." She said that she'd healed herself. "That's good, right? I don't know what happened to you, but you're not hurt, and that's very important."

"I've had a shitty couple of days, and I just want normal." She cried again, and he didn't blame her for being upset. "When will things stop happening to me, Colton? I'm sick of this shit."

"I am too, if it makes you feel any better. Tell me what had happened to you and what healed. Your dad said that I was go give him a full report. I'm assuming that you did tell him about your powers, correct?" She nodded and looked at her arm. "Did you break it, Hailey? Did you break your arm?"

"I cut it badly on the glass from the windshield. And my legs, both of them, were broken as well, and they just popped back into line and I could get up." He nodded while she looked terrified. "I had to lift the car up on my dad's side. I had to get him out before he was hurt worse. And I just lifted up the car, pulled him out, and set it back down. I was thinking that the police would need things to be the way they were so that they could make a good arrest. My body healed, and I lifted a car to get my dad out, and I was thinking of evidence. I'm insane."

Colton couldn't stop it, he burst out laughing at the way she had said it like it was something that she did daily. When she smacked him on the chest, he laughed harder. She was safe, and so was her father. That was all he cared about for the moment.

Wyatt and Dad came in a few minutes later. He told them both that she was fine, but to not act like it until she was home, so no one would know she'd healed. Dad started wrapping up her perfectly fine arm in gauze so that no one would react to her being healed.

"I want you to know how sorry I am about what I said to you the other day." Colton watched them both as his dad apologized to Hailey. "In addition to hurting your feelings, and I know that I did, I also intruded into things that were none of my business. You and Colton, that's who it was between, and I butted in. That is something that I'll never do again. You can count on it."

Hailey lifted his dad's face up so that she could look him in the eyes. Colton knew that she'd not hurt his dad, but he did wonder what she was going to say to him. Dad put his hand over hers and apologized again.

"You're a good father and a better man. You were only

81

protecting what was yours, and I cannot fault you for that. Please, let's not bring this up again, and move on as if it never happened." Dad nodded, but Colton knew that his dad would never forget. "I've had a shitty couple of weeks, as I sure you're well aware of. But having you talk to me, without fists or verbal insults, was the nicest way anyone has ever told me off in my life."

Dad laughed, and so did he and Wyatt. When they were satisfied that she looked as beaten up as they were going to get her, Dad wheeled her down the hall to see her dad. Colton sat on her bed and looked at his little brother.

"Don't say it. I don't want to hear from the peanut gallery today, or ever, if you don't mind." Colton laughed and asked him what he was talking about. "You know damn well what I'm talking about. Me having a mate soon. If you want to know the truth, I'm both terrified and excited. But the terror of a mate like the rest of you have scares the shit out of me."

"She may be a ball buster, as I've heard Brayden talk about the mates, but yours might be very soft spoken and sweet. Never says a curse word either." Wyatt stared at him as he held the bandage and the tape that he'd used. "This mystery woman might be so docile that the others will have fun with her."

"The others will eat her alive, and you fucking know it." They both laughed hard about his unknown mate. "I'm not so much set in my ways, but I do have things the way I want them. I have a house that I love working on. An expansive yard that means none of you are too close to bother me. And I've money in the bank."

"Yes, but that will matter shit when she comes here." Wyatt said he was thinking the same thing. "You'll love having a mate, Wyatt. They're the best thing you could ever imagine."

Colton went to find Hailey, leaving his brother in her room trying to wrap his head around whatever he thought of as a mate. Colton had a feeling that whatever he was thinking about, he wasn't going to be prepared for her. No one ever was when love hit them.

He stopped walking, and stood there for several seconds thinking about what he'd just thought about. Love. Colton was in love with his mate, and he wasn't sure he hadn't been long before today.

~*~

Hailey didn't know what to do in the house. Her dad had gone out to the yard when the gardener had shown up, and was, she was sure, bothering him. His arm was still in a sling, so she knew that he couldn't get into too much trouble. But Dad was having fun being here, and finding out that retired life was pretty good.

Going out onto the deck, just to get out of the house, she sat down on one of the pieces that she'd brought here from the other house. Hailey thought about Ray and the trouble that woman was having. Pulling out her cell phone, she called the store that she owned and wondered if she should be bothering her. She didn't get a chance to hang up before someone answered the phone. She was the phone service for Ms. Ray, the other woman said.

"Hi, my name is Hailey Whitehead. I was wondering, if she's not too busy, if I could speak to Ray? If she doesn't remember me, that's fine. I'll call back some other time." She was babbling and hated herself for that. When the phone was put on hold, Hailey was tempted just to hang up. "You're an idiot if you think a woman like her is going to remember an idiot like you. Hailey, I worry about you sometimes."

"Do you always talk to yourself? You should really try and be more positive rather than negative. It'll make you feel better in the long run. And yes, I remember you, Hailey. How could I forget the woman who punched my dad in the face?" Hailey let out a long breath and smiled. "How are you doing? I should have given you my number when David went with you. He has called me every night thanks to you giving him a cell phone."

"That's all right. I know that his dad might have been able to track him with something from you, so it was my pleasure to get him one. How are you doing otherwise?" Ray told her how her spring collection was giving her fits. "It's only summer — you know that, don't you?"

"Yes, I do. But I have to be two seasons ahead or I have nothing to send out for people to get excited about." They both laughed. "David said that you go and see him a few times a week. He also said that you've found yourself a mate in Colton. That's wonderful — you're a very lucky woman. My grandma just loved him to pieces."

"We're getting used to each other, I guess you could say. I'm not really the stay at home type, and I'm bored." Ray said that since she owned her own business, she was rarely if ever bored. "How is your grandma's house going? I saw all the equipment there when I picked up the last time. Were you able to get the last of your things out of there?"

"Oh yes. The barn is being dismantled now. I would have loved to do a room up with it — there are so many memories of that big place that I loved. But there is nowhere to have it put. I live in a condo that can barely hold me when I'm working." Hailey told her about the house that she was currently in and about the fire. "I heard about that from David. He said that it was a total loss. I'm so sorry to hear that, Hailey. If you need anything, let me know. I'm here for you, as you were for me that day. I'll never forget the look on my father's face when that wolf was on his chest."

"Yes, well, he deserved it. What a jackass." Hailey hoped that she wasn't keeping Ray from work and wondered how to get out of a call to the only person she knew that wasn't related to her. "David is doing well in school, by the way. I've had his math teacher work with him on what he's having issues with. He's a wonderful kid, as I'm sure you know."

"David and Grandma were all I had. And now she's gone. I don't know how I'm going to celebrate the holidays without her here. I would sneak down to see her and David when I could, but every holiday, I was there for sure." Hailey thought it terrible that Ray had to sneak anywhere and told her that. "My father is an ass, and spent money like he had an unlimited supply of it. He would take Grandma's checks and cash them, telling the bank he was doing it for her."

"I have a stepfather like that. He and my mom, I think they're the ones that burnt down dad's house and caused the accident that we were in." Ray told her what sort of things her dad had done in the name of money. "Do you think perhaps they might have come from the same devil's spawn? I think they might be related."

They both laughed, and Ray told her about the upcoming show that she was going to. It was in Vegas, and quite the best time she had working. Hailey told her that she'd seen a great deal of the country by driving, but never really got to visit the places.

"That's so sad. I've been everywhere. And now that I think about it, I've never visited places either. I was too busy making sure that there was a good line going out, and that the magazine

85

was perfect." She laughed, but it didn't sound like she found humor in her life. "Even on a date, I take calls and work from my phone. I guess that would explain why I don't date all that much."

They talked about this and that for another ten minutes. "Thank you for talking to me today. You've taken the boredom out of my day. I do hope that you have a fantastic show too."

"Thank you, Hailey. It's been a real pleasure talking to someone that isn't working for me and has no malicious reason for talking to me." Hailey told Ray that she was sorry that it was like that. "Its fine. I want us to get together. I'm going to come down to see David soon. And to finish up some paperwork that was left unfinished with my grandma passing. How about we spend the day together and catch up on anything but our sour lives?"

"I'd very much like that."

Hailey looked out beyond the trees and could see movement. Not really worried, she and Ray exchanged phone numbers and email addresses before hanging up.

Getting up slowly, she looked harder into the woods. It wasn't a wolf, and she was suddenly worried for her dad. He was in the yard still, and she could only hope that he was with the gardener and not roaming around where someone could hurt him. Stepping off the deck, the big cougar came more out of the woods and stood there as if waiting for her to make the next move. Taking a few steps toward the big beast, she started talking.

"I don't know who you are. And while I'm well aware that I live with a cougar and his family members are cougars too, I still don't know who the fuck you are. Either show yourself or I'm going to practice the fucked up things I can do on you." He didn't move, nor did he come at her. "You're really going to stand here and let me cut you to ribbons? I'm serious, buster. Show yourself."

He went from beast to man in seconds. Whoever he was, he screamed loudly and like he was in a great deal of pain. When he stood up, naked as the day he was born, Hailey thought about her hands and made one of them into a weapon, as hers was in the house.

The first shot she fired had him stepping back. She had shot right between his feet, and warned him again about fucking with her. Hailey didn't have any idea how to reach for anyone of the family but Colton, so she thought of all of them, including the mom and dad.

I'm in deep shit here. Colton asked what was going on—she could hear the concern in his voice. *There is a cougar on the land, currently standing naked in the field about ten yards from me. He won't speak, and he doesn't seem to care that I have a gun.*

Brayden said that he was close, and Wyatt said that he was on his way, he was at Mom and Dad's and was coming with him. Hailey felt better but knew that she was far from safe just yet. When a large hawk landed in front of her, the shift from bird to woman had her sighing with relief. It was Dane.

"Hello, shit for brains. Have you a death warrant or something? I'm pretty sure that she told you to stand down." Hailey held her gun steady as he took several steps toward her and Dane, halving the distance between them. Hailey fired again, hitting the man in the shoulder. "Mother fuck, you're good with that thing. Can you tell me, please, that you were aiming for his shoulder, and not, I don't know, for his tiny dick?"

Hailey said shoulder, but she was too scared now to bother

with the joke. When the man stood up, coming toward them again, Hailey wasn't sure what to do until she felt someone behind her. Without thinking of her own wellbeing, knowing that Dane had the guy should he come any closer, she turned and fired at the same time, hitting this man in the forehead when she didn't know him either. With the second sound of gunfire, Hailey knew that Dane had dispatched the first man.

She fell to the ground. Hailey was sick of killing people and told that to Dane. "I just want to live a normal, quiet life. And how the hell was I to know that telling someone that I was bored would bring this fucking shit to my door?"

"There is no such thing as normal or quiet with this family. And if you just wait a minute or two longer for Colton to get here, I think you'll find that he's going to be all over you. And not in a bad way." Hailey looked up at Dane and she winked at her. "They weren't after you, just so you know. But me. I'm cat shit in their sandbox, and they don't care for me in it. I'm going to teach you how to read minds when this is cleaned up. All right?"

"What about the other shit? Can you give me at least a little training on that too?" She said it would be her pleasure. "I'm afraid that I'm going to make Colton all the more nervous. I don't feel so well."

She fell back, blackness taking her under. She'd killed a man — another man — and Hailey had had enough.

Chapter 7

Linda couldn't understand her daughter. She didn't like her, but she was hers. She supposed that she could have been a better mother to her. Giving her a place to stay and whatnot when she'd come home. But who knew that she was going to be this fucking nerd that made money off of shit that she thought up? She looked at her other daughter and wondered if she'd be anything but the brat that she was. Probably not.

Shelly wasn't showing any kind of aptitude for learning anything other than her name. By the time that Hailey had been Shelly's age, she not only knew how to read and write, but she had taken to reading the dictionary, of all things. Hailey told her that she wanted to know every word there was and how to use them. What a total waste of time, she'd thought then, and now.

Going to the window of their hotel room, she was glad that the kids had taken a nap. Of course, she had given them a little something to make them sleep, hoping that it would give her a little peace. Linda wondered what Hailey would say, but she didn't care. She was cooped up in this small space, and needed to be able to have a thought that was her own.

Hailey had taken their thunder away. That was why Howard wasn't here—he'd gone to the newspaper to find out who had done this to them. Someone had taken it upon themselves not only to tell the world how she was this smart person that had invented all sorts of things, but that she was a hero too.

The headline was right there on the front page. There wasn't a picture of her, but the person didn't seem to need one the way he'd described her. Linda knew it was a man—there wasn't any way that someone could talk about Hailey like that and be a woman. Linda knew just how beautiful her daughter had grown up to be.

It mentioned Nelson's, and how they'd taken one of her inventions and used it for things that she'd not made it for. Howard thought that was a lie, that there wasn't any way that *dumbass Hailey* had invented anything. But Linda knew better.

Hailey was forever building things that worked, taking all kinds of scraps that she'd get from dumpsters and such to do it with. She made drawings that would make Linda dizzy when she looked at them. And calculations that Linda was sure that she'd never be able to figure out, even with a calculator. But Hailey knew. And she'd hidden them from her and Howard. That was one of the reasons they'd kicked her out. Howard was sure, and had assured Linda, that Hailey was making a bomb to kill them all.

There was the money too. The card that they got money on each month had fed them nicely at the beginning. But by the end of the month, when the card was empty, they'd be eating buttered noodles and peanut butter and jelly sandwiches. Linda was never eating that shit again after they had money.

But the paper had come out, telling Hailey's whole life story on two pages of it. They'd left nothing out, other than to not mention Linda or Howard's name. Secretly she thought that was the reason that Howard had been so mad; she'd not mentioned any of her second family.

Going out the door and sitting on the chairs that had been there when they arrived, Linda took a deep clean breath and remembered how much she loved living in this part of the country. The air was cleaner than when she'd been home. There wasn't as much traffic screaming by them at every turn. And she could see the stars at night when she got a minute to herself, she could see them.

Linda heard rather than saw Howard coming back from wherever he'd been. The car that they were driving was as old as dirt and ran like shit. The muffler had fallen off on the drive here, and the tires were so bald that she was sure that she could see her reflection in them. When he turned the engine off, she put her fingers in her ears waiting for the loud noise to stop. She thought it was showing how pissed it was because no one was caring for it.

She could tell by the way that Howard slammed the door when he got out that nothing had gone his way. She wondered what they'd do now. Hailey wouldn't be giving them money for blackmailing her now. That she thought they could bank on.

"Some reporter did it. They said that their name was on the article. I had to go buy a stupid paper to read that since they wouldn't just tell me. Some fucker by the name of L. Mossrose. Whoever heard of a name like that?"

"I suppose we should head home then. You know as well as I do that was the only reason that we had for her to pay us." He said they weren't leaving until they had the cash. "All right, but what are we going to use that's not already out there? I'm all game. I don't know what we might find once we get home — we might not even have a place to go by then."

She was as sure about that as she was that Howard loved her. Their landlord had left messages with her friend that lived next door to her. Linda either cleaned up the yard and the toys that were broken all over the grass, or she was gone. People should look at it as her kids having fun rather than making a mess. Linda hated everyone as much as she did her ex-husband. He had been a stick in the mud about every little thing she'd done when she'd been with him.

Peter had known that Hailey wasn't his. He'd known about Linda's affairs, too. But when Hailey had been born he had treated her no different than he had Pete. Maybe even a little better. That was why she'd wanted Hailey to be with her after the divorce, because Peter had loved her too much. And a fat lot of good that had done her, too. Hailey had ended up with him anyway, plotting and working to disgrace her.

That wouldn't have been hard, she knew. The things that she'd done to Hailey should have gotten her a long prison term. But the stupid girl either didn't care or she was too dumb to realize that she could call the police on her.

"Are you even listening to me, Linda?" She smiled at Howard, being ripped from her thoughts when he shook her hard enough to feel her teeth move. "I was trying to tell you of my plan. But you were off in some other land. Were you thinking of ways to get some cash from that kid of yours too?"

"Yes, as a matter of fact I have been. Did you hear that she got married?" It had been all the girls at the convenience store could talk about, how another Stanton was off the market. Whoever the hell they were. "She's supposed to have met him recently and they fell madly in love, or some bullshit. Anyway, the women that I heard talking about it, they said that he'd just gotten a windfall in this big lot of furniture from some rich woman who died and left it to him. I asked, and it's just old stuff that nobody really wants. But there might have been a little money in it. I thought we could take her or Peter and have these Stantons give us some cash for them to come back. Then after that, we could burn that house down too."

"Brilliant. I love that idea. And it won't be considered kidnapping because it's your daughter and ex-husband. This is going to work. But we have to figure out a way to make sure that she pays up this time." He grinned at her after kissing her twice. "And if she dares telling us no again, we'll make sure she knows just how easy it was to take her loved ones."

They made plans to find out where this Stanton lived, but it was impossible to figure out which Stanton she'd married. There were about a dozen of them in the directory, counting businesses and other shit. They thought about calling to ask if it was her husband but didn't know that many phone numbers. The local directory that the town put out only said names and addresses, no phone numbers.

Finally, they decided to narrow it down to one. She was sure that was it, Wyatt Stanton. He was a doctor—well, all of them were—but she had a feeling with a name like Wyatt, he'd be desperate enough to marry Hailey. She was a freak, after all, with being so smart.

The kids started to wake up and realized that they'd not gotten anything for dinner. Howard wanted to splurge, but there wasn't anything to splurge with. Not even a little squirt. But he convinced her that it was a done deal, and they ordered a pizza and even had it delivered. That was all the money now.

They didn't even have a nickel to their names.

But the kids were happy about the treat, and she was too. One less thing she'd have to do in cleaning up. They had told the motel office that they'd feel better about cleaning the room on their own, and would come for towels when they needed them. Having a hot plate as well as the other cooking items they had would have gotten them kicked out. As it was, they were avoiding the manager because of the bill mounting up.

She was sort of nervous about this. Linda wasn't backing out of it—it was an excellent plan—but she was nervous about them getting caught. There was no way that this wasn't an illegal way to get money. But Howard had never steered her wrong, and second guessing him this late in the game was just stupid. Especially since nearly all his plans before had gone through without a hitch.

Leaving the kids in the bed, Linda locked the door and got in the car with Howard. He didn't speak—he'd told her that when they were going with a plan, he needed absolute quiet before it happened. Left to her own thoughts, she looked back on the first time they'd blackmailed Hailey.

Linda had been sitting at the table, just relaxing while the kids had gone down the street to play with the other kids in the neighborhood. She seldom got a few minutes to herself anymore, and when school had finished up for the year, she got to be alone less and less.

The newspaper in their town hadn't been much. About twenty pages that mostly consisted of games from around the country, some obits that she rarely read, and a few other things that really didn't interest her. But having the few minutes, it had been something that she did, just so she'd not have to look at the mess the house had always been in.

The name Whitehead had popped out at her. She didn't know if it was the same family as hers, but she had been surprised to find out that not only was it her daughter, but that she'd made a great deal of money on some shit that she'd invented.

The paper had gone on and on about how she was a philanthropist, that she was brilliant and other shit. But it was the money that she was most interested in. The other thing, philanthropist, was where she'd figured out that she was giving away her inventions that helped people. Her daughter had turned into a sap.

"She might as well be giving it to us." Linda had agreed with Howard, and they'd both decided to make a few calls about her and see what they could dig up. They'd talked to some reporter, who had told them the juiciest details about her.

"My editor told me to sit on it. The woman does a lot of things for people, and he and I agreed that it would make her look bad. And the money would stop flowing from her. While I do agree with him, I worked hard on this shit." Linda told him that she could see it in the article. "Thanks. You said she was your daughter? I tell you, she's about the sweetest person that I've met. And really upfront about what she had a part in."

"What sort of part is that? I mean, we're not speaking to each other these days. You know how kids can be." Linda had had to think hard as to how old Hailey would have been then. "We'll get back together soon. I'm her best friend most of the time, but a boyfriend got between us, and I'm hoping she sees reason."

Linda had also known that her daughter wouldn't have been dating at all after what her and Howard had done to her. That had been the greatest money maker for them in the beginning, and the biggest disaster that they'd ever had when it was over. Once she'd been released by the men they'd sold her to, they had demanded their money back. Linda had hated Hailey for that.

But when they'd heard about her part in the scandal at Nelson's, they'd jumped on that like white on rice. It took them longer to find a working number for Hailey than it did for them to look up what had happened, and why that guy had been sitting on the story. After that, it had been easy living for a while.

Hailey had forked over five grand in a heartbeat. She didn't want her poor old dad brought into it. And that, as they say, had been their way to get more from her. Hailey loved her dad, and Linda and Howard had held that over her head for the next five years. But now, it seemed that she didn't care.

When Howard said that they were there, she stared at the big house, tearing herself away from her thoughts. They thought this was the one that belonged to her daughter, but it had to be worth about a million dollars. Christ, it looked like a fucking hotel it was so big. She wondered what kind of doctor Hailey's new hubby was and decided that he was someone that made women look better. A plastic surgeon. He'd be rolling in the dough with that sort of business.

"Okay, I'm going to go to the door and you go around back, like we planned. I'm sure a dumb fucker that owns a house like this never thinks that anyone is going to try and come in. Security isn't necessary when you can buy every little thing you want." Linda told him again that she didn't want to go in the back door. "You have to. If they figure out you're her mom, and you look like her enough to say that, then he might just slam the door in your face. There is no telling what Hailey has told him.

All of it might be true, but it won't get us what we want."

Okay, he had a point there. Getting out, she made her way to the back of the house, and was discouraged that the fucker had put a high fence around the place. Even jumping as high as she could, there wasn't any way that she could see in, much less get in. And walking all the way around it, she figured out that there was no entrance to the yard.

She made her way to the front again just in time to see Howard running as if his life depended on it. Linda wondered what had happened when she heard the low growl from behind her. Turning slowly so as not to spook what she thought was a dog, she nearly fainted dead away when she saw the fucking huge wolf, with teeth that looked to be as big as her fucking arm. Linda almost beat Howard to the car, she was so scared.

~*~

Wyatt laughed every time he thought of Hailey's parents being chased off his property. Even the mom, when she'd walked around the house, didn't know that he was right behind her the entire way. When he'd gotten to the front, leaving the pack of wolves that roamed the land, he saw Howard, wet pants and all, running from Carl, one of the pack that he'd just left.

"You want to share with me what you find so funny, Dr. Stanton?" He told his nurse, Sarah, another wolf friend, what had happened last night. "Oh my. I wish I could have seen that. I can't believe that wonderful woman Hailey is a part of that family. I love her father, he's such a sweet man. Did I tell you that he stopped to help my mom when her car broke down? And wouldn't take anything for it, either."

"He is a good man. He and my dad sit for long hours, Mom told me, just talking about life and bullshitting like it's a sport and the one with the biggest tale wins. They have been coming up with some pretty farfetched fibs, too." Wyatt wondered aloud why they'd been at his house. "I mean, I understand that they'd not have any idea who I am, but why are they going to any of our houses? You think they have been planning? Hailey said that they were good at making plans, but not so good at making them work for themselves."

"There are all kinds of idiots around, and I think they are the worst kind. Imagine trying to blackmail their own child. Why, you'd think they'd be singing her praises from what I've read about her. And the other day when she was here, she was just as nice as pie. However, she and Dane, they can sure outdo each other, don't you think?" Wyatt laughed and said that he thought so as well. "Well, we have three more to see today, and I think that'll be it. Unless something comes up, you're going to be done by five o'clock today."

"How many times have you said that to me, and at five minutes to five, I get an emergency?" They both laughed, and Sarah went to answer the phone when it rang. Wyatt had a feeling that his leaving on time notion was out the window.

He was just working on some way to win at the solitaire game he was playing when Sarah told him he had a phone call. Wyatt had seen the last of his patients today, and even had one extra. Today was turning out to be a good day, and he was sure that whoever was calling him was going to call him away. Laughing, he answered the phone.

"Is this Doctor Stanton?" He said that he was one of them and asked who he was looking for. "I don't know his name. Just that he's a Stanton. I'd like to speak to the one that just got married. We, uh, we have a surprise for him and his bride for their marriage thing."

"Marriage thing? No, I'm not going to tell you which one

has just gotten married in a married thing." The man huffed and told him to hold on. When he must have put his hand over the receiver to talk to someone else, he reached out to Hailey to let her know that her parents were looking for her. When the man came back on the line, Wyatt told him that he was too busy to be put on hold again. "I have people to see and things to do."

"Why are you all doctors?" The man sounded very perplexed about that, but Wyatt didn't enlighten him. Wyatt was ready to tell him off when he heard back from Hailey.

I'm assuming that you haven't told them anything. He said that he hadn't, it was just too much fun to have them guessing. *Yes, well, you might not have thought it was fun if they had gotten into your house. Though, I haven't the foggiest idea why they were doing that.*

I would imagine that they were hoping that you were home, at my house, and that you'd be easy pickings in the middle of the night. She laughed, but he could tell she was strained about this thing. *They didn't bother me, and the pack hasn't had that much fun chasing someone in months.*

I know, but I can't help but worry about who they might try to target next. I'd have gone to the courthouse to get the information, but I doubt very much that either of them would have a clue how to do that. He told her about the "marriage thing." *Oh, brother. I tell you, I think that Howard is as dumb as a post. I was just wondering who was watching their kids. Or did they just leave them at the hotel?*

Wyatt hadn't thought of that. The children hadn't been with them when they'd been at his house. He might have to call Children's Services soon if they were doing that. He asked Hailey if she'd have a problem with that when Howard started talking again.

"Hello, are you still there? I think he hung up on me, Linda."

Wyatt told him he was there, but extremely busy and to get to the point. "I want to congratulate the happy couple is all."

"You said that you had a gift for them. Now you just want to congratulate them? What is the deal here? Who are you?" The line went dead, and he laughed harder.

Wyatt knew that this was serious business. He was well aware that someone might get hurt before this was done. But for now, he'd keep the others informed of the call, as well as see if the pack could roam all their properties a little more.

No, I don't have a problem with that. But I'm telling you upfront. If someone contacts me to take the kids in, they can stop that shit right now. They're heathens, and I would send them to military school just so that someone else could try and beat some sense into their heads. He told her that he might help them after the other day. *Yes, well, they're monsters. And I know that it isn't kind to talk about children that way when it is their parents' fault that they're like that, but I think that everyone would agree that they're not your usual kids.*

He told her he didn't think so either, and then told her that he'd keep her informed. After closing down his game after realizing that he wasn't going to win this one, Wyatt leaned back in his chair and closed his eyes for a moment.

Colton and he were very close. He had no idea if it was because they'd become doctors, though different kinds, that they had a bond that none of the rest of them had. But last night, talking to him, Wyatt wanted to either bash his head in or feel sorry for him. He'd not touched Hailey since they'd moved in together.

"She's stressed out." Wyatt pointed out that sex could relieve some of that. "Yes, but she doesn't trust me. And I only just figured out that I'm in love with her."

"Yeah, well, we all could see that." Colton asked him why

he'd not told him. "Because we all figured, I guess, that you'd be smart enough to know that already. Christ, Colton, tell her that you love her, and convince her that she can trust you. I'm sure by now that she's figured that part out."

"I don't know if she has or not, actually. I can see that she's beginning to, but it's like all my studies have gone out the window where she is concerned. I can't fix this." Wyatt told him that he should figure out a way to tell her what she meant to him. "Then what? Do I try and jump her bones? I'm telling you right now, I'm a little afraid of what she can do. Dane has been working with her on some of it, and she told me that Hailey is indeed as powerful as she is, and can do everything, and I mean every little thing, that Dane can do."

"So? She can protect you when it comes down to it. Unless that's what's bothering you." Colton assured him that it wasn't. He didn't care who did the saving, so long as they got to go home at the end of the day. "I don't know what to tell you. I think that I'd just lay it all out there and let her know just how you feel. But then I'm not you. You're more of the pussy type when it comes to confrontations and all."

"I most certainly am not." They both laughed then. "I'm going to ask her out. Take her someplace nice, with cloth napkins instead of the kind that you get from a dispenser that everyone uses."

"Good. Now, this session is only going to cost you ten grand."

Colton had left him after that, telling him that he was going to be making plans to blow her out of the water. For some reason, Wyatt didn't think that was what she'd wanted, romance. It didn't seem to be something that would have her all mushy and turned on. He thought that she was more the kind that would enjoy a nice fishing trip. Thinking of that, Wyatt called his dad and asked if he wanted to drown some worms. Dad, of course, was all for it. Dad rarely turned down time to spend with any of them.

Plans made, he watched the clock more now. A fishing trip with his dad — it was going to be just what he needed. His dad was the best there was at making a person, especially his sons, feel on top of the world.

At one second after five he was nearly to his car. Laughing at how he felt like he'd won something, Wyatt stopped at the deli for big beefy subs and a couple of bottles of pop. They didn't drink it often, so it was a treat. Getting back into his car, he was on his way to the lake. Good times were going to be had by both of them.

Chapter 8

Colton was standing in the florist shop when he realized this was a mistake. She might just shove roses up his nose for being so dense, or she'd shove them up his nose because they were cut flowers and not plants. Looking around the shop, he realized also that this wasn't what he wanted. He wanted her to trust him. That was all, because he knew that if she trusted him, then everything else would fall into place. At least that was his theory.

Going through downtown, he saw his brother coming out of the deli. That sounded good. Thick Italian subs with some pickle chips. He detoured around and was headed into the place that Wyatt had left to figure out what she might like. Then it occurred to him. Just ask her.

Hey, are you busy? She told him that she was working with Dane, but they were about done. *I was going to pick up some subs for dinner. I realized that I have no idea what you might like. I, myself, enjoy a nice Italian one without hot peppers. What can I get you?*

Oh, Colton, that sounds wonderful. Yes, a sub. I would love an

Italian too, but with the hot peppers and also pepper jack cheese. If you get them cold, we can heat them up here and they'll be ten times better. Remembering that her dad was living with them, he asked what Peter would like, disappointed that they'd not be alone. *He's gone to look at houses. He said that he wants his own place. The insurance company paid him today. I'm so glad. He's just waiting on the one for his business to see how that goes.*

Mentally rubbing his hands together, he got what she wanted and his order too. He would have to remember that she liked her food hot. It really wasn't a surprise to him, as heated as she was making him. After picking up a nice blueberry pie and ice cream, he was on his way home. This was going to be fun.

He wasn't entirely sure how this was going to make her trust him, but it was going to be fun just spending time with her. Peter usually left them to whatever they were doing in the evening in favor of going to his room. He had time to read now, and he was enjoying some of the classics that he'd not read in a while.

Peter had become a good friend of his father, and most times they'd be out and about around town. He was sure that Dad had introduced him to everyone, and the man seemed to be well received. Wyatt had told Peter and Hailey both what had happened at his home, and he was glad to have seen that it was funny to them and not stressful.

Pulling his car into the garage, he noticed the addition right away. He'd bet anything that is was the same car that Hailey and her dad had been working on. Wondering where it might have been that didn't have it in the garage, he bypassed it to head into the house. He walked into the kitchen just as Hailey was pulling her shirt over her head.

He couldn't move. Well, he could move, but was afraid of the direction that he might be headed. Colton had promised her that they'd not be having sex until she wanted it, but right now, he couldn't seem to focus on anything but her beautiful bare skin that seemed to scream at him to be touched. Before he could begin to talk himself out of just touching her, he had his hand on her skin that the shirt hadn't yet fallen over.

"Your skin, it's much softer than I thought it would be. And trust me, I've been thinking about it a great deal."

She turned to his body and he could see her face. Desire was there. Need almost as strong as his own. Pulling her closer to him, it was like touching a match to a gallon of gasoline. It was explosive. Christ, she was touching him everywhere she could reach.

Picking her up so that her legs were wrapped around his hips, he took her to the counter as he devoured her mouth. She tasted of spring, a warm breeze, and sex all at the same time. As soon as her ass touched the counter, she pulled away from him and ripped the buttons off his shirt. Before he could do the same to her, get her naked as fast as he could, Hailey bit down on his nipple and nearly sent him over the edge of consciousness.

No words were needed right now. His mind would focus on one thing at a time, and when that was done, he'd think of something else. Having her here, with him like this, it was hard to breathe much less think beyond having her under him.

When she cupped his cock through his pants, he rolled into her hand. His pants were the next thing to go as she pulled the button off and tore the zipper in half. Christ, he was ready to come right now, just getting naked with her. He was going to surely die when he was inside of her.

"Hurry, Colton." He wasn't sure what she wanted him

to do—hurrying was what he was doing—but when he slid his hands down the back of her shorts, she cried out when he ripped them off her, panties included. "Yes, please. I need you. I want to feel you when you take me."

"I want to taste you." She nodded, then shook her head. "Baby, I'm barely holding on here—what do you want?"

"Everything." Colton nodded—he was sure that he could do that for her. Kissing her again, he pulled his boxers down with his torn pants. Colton looked into her eyes as he slid slowly into her heat. "Colton. I'm going to come."

Her scream had him taking her. His plan, if there had been one, was to give her as much pleasure as he could before taking his own. But the moment that she cried out his name, Colton didn't hold back. He took her hard enough that things started to fall from the cabinets around them.

Picking her up again, he lifted her up and down while he moved to the nearest wall. Fucking her, taking her there, seemed just as dangerous as the counter had been. Colton gave up and took her to the floor then. He was so close to coming inside of her that he could actually see stars.

Her body was made for his. He touched her everywhere he could reach, tasting her flesh as he sampled every inch of her. And when she bowed up from the floor, her body pressing harder into his, he watched her climax and fell more in love with her than he'd ever dreamed possible.

When she dug her nails into his back, he moved his mouth along her throat. It was heated there, the blood just on the surface, waiting for him to drink. And when he bit down, feeling his own climax race to the finish line, he felt his cat run over him just as he let go of a roar that seemed to come from his feet.

He needed more, needed to take her in a way that would have him and his cat satisfied. Sitting up, he turned her over and had her get on her knees as he pounded inside of her. Colton grabbed onto her hair, holding onto her. When she screamed out that she was coming again, his second climax rolled from his body like a freight train leaving the station.

Colton leaned over her and bit down hard on her shoulder. The taste of her, the richness of her blood, made him light headed one second, then he felt the power that was hers roll through him. Christ, he wondered if she felt like this all the time. If so, he could almost envy her this.

When she fell forward after he sadly left her body, it was all he could do not to fall on her and smash her into the floor. Colton took them both to the floor, this time her on top of him as they both seemed to be working hard at catching their breaths. When she rolled over so that she was facing him, Colton asked her if she was all right.

"No, I don't think I ever will be again, thanks to you." He grinned at her, and felt like a man on top of the world. "Please tell me that you enjoyed that. I'm know that sounds like I'm asking you for praise or something, but I've not had a lot of luck with sexual partners in the past."

"I don't think that I'm going to be able to move for the rest of my life. You, my dear, drained me to the point of not knowing if the cook is going to come in tomorrow and find me lying here with a very happy smile on my face." She sat up, and he helped her to slide over him. "I could have sworn that I was done, but having you ride me it's a treat that I'd enjoy even if you were to do that again."

"You feel so good like this. Like I can explore you, touch you like you belong to me." Colton nearly told her that he did belong to her, but she spoke before he could. "I'm not sure what it was that had you breaking your promise not to make love to me. But if I tell you to bring home subs every night, can I have that again?"

She rolled her hips over his. Colton wanted her to both slow down, take her time, as much as he needed her to peak, so that he could watch her beautiful face when she did. Holding her hips, squeezing them when she hit a spot on him that made him want to beg, Colton asked her if she was upset with him.

"No. Not at all. I've been thinking of ways to get you in the sack for days now. I want to taste you like you did me. Bite your throat and feel the difference in my body when you let me come with you." The change of subject was quick, but not enough that he didn't want to tell her anyway. "I'm so close to coming, Colton. Help me. Please?"

He sat up and took her breast into his mouth. She was slim in her body, but her breasts were full and responsive. As he suckled at one then the other, he held her to him as she rode him faster. When she was close—he could hear the difference in her heartbeat—he rolled her to the floor again and took her the way he'd wanted to before. Slow and easy.

"I do belong to you." She shook her head. "Oh, but I do. I cannot tell you how much I've fallen in love with you. Tell you that you have taken my heart and made it your own. Hailey, I cannot breathe without having your scent. Feel when you aren't sharing with me. I've fallen in love with you."

"You just want to get laid." Colton kissed her then, hearing the panic in her voice, feeling her shyness as she tried to push him away mentally. "Colton, I'm not the kind of woman people fall in love with. I'm what most would consider damaged goods. Haven't you been listening to me tell you what's going on with me? I'm a mess, and I don't think that it'll get any better."

"I love your mess of a life. I want to be there for you, not taking over, but for you whenever you need me to be. Having you as my mate, it's made me appreciate my brothers and their love for their mates." He suckled on her breast and moaned when she did. "I want to come inside of you, feel it when your body ripples like a waterfall over me. Come for me, love. Come for us both to be complete."

He didn't know what to expect from her. Would she push him away, tell him to fuck off? But then she bared her throat for him, giving over to him everything that he desired within her. Hailey cried out when he licked the warmed skin over her pulse and held him to her when she came again, this time with him drinking from her even as he filled her with himself.

Hailey moved under him, and he lifted his head from her shoulder and looked down at her. She'd fainted this time, her body surging up off the floor as he sealed up the wound that he'd made. Now looking down at her, Colton could have sworn that he was the only man in the world that had a mate like his right now. In fact, he was sure of it.

This time when he rolled to his back, he stood up and reached for her, giving her a hand up as he thought of what they'd just done. Asking her if she was all right, she nodded and told him that she was going to get her a shirt. Colton nearly told her that she was fine the way she was when he realized that she was embarrassed.

Following her, he watched as she sorted through the laundry that had been washed yesterday. "You could just think of dressing yourself. I'm sure that you can do that as well." Nodding, she kept looking in the basket instead of at him. "Hailey, I can't fix what I don't know. I don't want you to hold back on me if there was something that I've done to hurt you in any way."

"I didn't think it would be like this." He asked her like what. "You. Me. Falling in love. I have known for a few days that's what I felt for you. But I'd made this deal with you—a stupid one now that I've nearly raped you—but it was a deal that I had no idea how to go back on."

"Did you show me your back to get me started? I have to tell you, it worked." She glanced at him and he could tell that hadn't been her plan. "I don't care how we came together. I really don't. But I'm in love with you too. We're going to be all right from now on."

Holding her in his arms when she came to him, Colton thought of clothing and wasn't really surprised that he was dressed. When she looked up at him, pulling away just enough to look, he kissed her deeply and told her he was starving.

The subs had survived, barely. But once they were heated up and cut in half, the two of them joked and tossed food at one another as they grew comfortable with each other. He loved her, she loved him. Colton didn't care what came next involving her parents. He was ready to battle them at this moment because Hailey trusted him.

~*~

Howard was still nursing the cut on his leg. Christ, there was a pack of wolves on Hailey's land, and he was sure that she'd had something to do with one of them biting him. As he wrapped the torn sheet around his calf again, he limped out of the bathroom to see if Linda was faring any better than he was.

"They tried to eat me." He told her that he knew that. "They tried to eat us, Howard. What kind of fucked up mess is that? Those damned animals tried to fucking eat me."

110

"But they didn't, and we're going to be prepared for them the next time." She asked him how. "I have a plan that will knock them out as quickly as it does the kids when we give them something. We'll have to spend some money, though."

"There isn't any money. None at all. Even our secret *in case stash* is gone. If we don't get some money soon, we're going to be found in this room starving and eating our children." He thought that was a little overboard, but he understood her concern. "I had to give the kids crackers and water for breakfast and lunch. They're not going to put up with that much longer, Howard. They're as hungry as we are."

He wondered if they could keep them drugged until they had some cash but dismissed that. There might be a long-term effect on the stuff they were giving the kids, and he didn't want to have to take care of a retarded one. It would cost money, he thought, and until they got ahold of Hailey, there wasn't any to be had.

"I'm going to have to break down and try and call her." He looked at Linda and asked her why she'd want to do that. "We're hungry."

He didn't care for the way she shouted at him. What did she think, that he wasn't starving too? But before he could ask her that question, there was someone pounding on the door.

Howard was glad now that they'd given the kids a little extra to make them sleep. Christ, it was imperative that whoever was on the other side of the door wouldn't wake them up anyway. That would surely give them away, especially if they were asking for money. It was too soon for them to come by and demand money anyway. They'd had no chance of getting to Hailey yet.

The pounding seemed to go on forever. But when they

finally quit, he waited a full minute before he braved the curtain and looked in the parking lot. He had to look really hard to read the name on the side of the big van, and when he fell back, not believing what he was seeing, he knew they were going to be in deep fucking shit if these people were to get ahold of the children right now.

"It's Child Services. Someone sicced them on us." He whispered in the event that someone was still out there waiting for them to make a noise. "Who would even know that we have kids in here but the fucking owner of this dive? I have a good mind to go up there and beat the crap out of him for this."

"Do you know what would have happened had they seen them right now?" He nodded, terrified more than he wanted to admit. "They would have jailed us. Fucking shit, Howard, why would he do that to us? Sure, we owe them some money, but that ain't no cause for them to get our kids taken from us. If the people in charge were to know that our kids were being doped up, they'd surely make us pay in some ways that would hurt us more."

They sat there by the window for another hour, waiting to see if the van left or someone just broke down the door. It wouldn't surprise him if that fucking guy who was renting them this dive of a hotel room would laugh about getting them in trouble. They needed to get in touch with Hailey now, not later.

"I think you should go with your plan about calling her." Linda nodded, her face pale because of recent events. "We have to make her understand that she has to give us some money now. We need it to get our kids something to eat and better drugs to make them be quiet. Do you think you can find a number for her? Soon?"

"I don't know, Howie, but I sure will give it my best." He knew that she would. It was important for them both that this work out the way that they wanted. "I'll see what I can find out tomorrow. Those women at the convenience store, they'll probably know how to call that guy."

They didn't know what to do. There wasn't any way that they were going to leave the place now. Not with those guys lurking around, just waiting for them to leave the kids alone again. What the hell did they expect them to do when they were out running around trying to get Hailey to pay them? Take them with them? Heavens to Betsy, that would be a disaster. He knew it. They'd be whining the entire time about how hungry they were, and he'd had about enough of that.

Getting up from the floor when he saw that the van was gone, he still kept his voice down just in case. He hugged Linda and told her that it would be all right. She'd contact Hailey and have her meet her someplace, and they'd take her. Surely her new husband would pay to get her back. Howard asked Linda if she thought he would.

"I don't know, Howie, I just don't. Things aren't going the way we need them to go. Not one bit." He told her that he'd noticed that as well. "But I can hope on the fact that she's gotten on his last nerve the way she used to us when she would spout off information. It was like she had the book in front of her."

She had known a great many things that had irritated them. The fact that she'd read a law book once was what got her shut out of the house. That and the fact that they were both afraid that she was smarter than them. She was, but they were horrified that she was going to realize it and start running things her way.

It was about seven when Linda went to the store. She

didn't have any money with her, thanks to him wanting a hot pizza, and he knew now that he shouldn't have done that. But it didn't lessen the fact that they were broke now. Linda had worn her shopping shirt and skirt, and he knew they'd at least have something besides crackers when she got back.

Howard thought about the way things had gone with Linda's daughter. He knew that she wasn't Peter's girl. And the fact that Linda had no idea who might be the father kinda made him feel superior to Hailey.

The girl was just too much of everything. Too smart. Always wanting to take a shower and wash her hair. If you weren't planning on going somewhere, why bother with even combing your hair? If you weren't going out, then no one would remark on how shitty you looked. But she apparently did, and he had always been glad when she went back to school.

What they'd not counted on when they'd kicked her out was how much money she was going to be making later. All they could see was that without her there, the food card went a good deal further. Then there was the bankruptcy thing.

He'd filed the right paperwork to get the creditors off their back. Yes, they had bought more than their asses could pay for, but that wasn't his fault. He had been sucked in by the card company and had gotten way over his head before he could stop it from tumbling down on them.

Howie had gotten all his shit together and was just getting ready to get the check when the banker had called and said that it was all canceled. Then he hung up, not a word on why, just canceled. After Howie had done all that work, too.

Two days later the welfare people had shown up with all kinds of documentation that proved that they'd been getting support for someone that wasn't living with them. He knew that it had been Hailey — just knew that she'd done this to them. Christ almighty, she'd sure messed things up for them.

Not only did they lose their nice four-bedroom house, but also their card and the free lunches that the kids got at school. But the real kicker was when the health department had told them that their health card wasn't good anymore. How was he supposed to get his teeth fixed up if they took that? And it wasn't as if they'd been getting anything from them for Hailey. It was a service that they'd gotten for free.

He watched the kids sleeping for a few minutes and wondered why they'd had them. It wasn't as if they had all that much to give them. He and Linda had wanted to go on grand adventures, have some fun. But again, Hailey had messed that up too. Not Linda getting pregnant, but simply by the fact that they had nothing that paid them for the kids — that really pissed him off. The more kids they had, he'd heard from his buddy, the more the government had to fork over.

Howard knew that there were some people that really needed it. He could have gotten a job, he supposed. Helped to keep his family clothed and fed. But there was so much more shit that you got by not working than there was for working. He'd figured that one out the month that the government found out he had a job and cut the food card money in half. There was a valuable lesson in that. All work was a killer, all play got you paid. He told that to his kids every day.

The key in the lock had him tensing up. He just knew it was going to be the landlord coming by for cash. But it was only Linda, and boy oh boy, had she done well at the store. They'd be eating good now. With all that she'd gotten them, hell, they might have to hit two stores at once, both with their shopping clothes on.

They pigged out on the pizzas and candy bars with the kids. Then after they were stuffed, they had a burping contest while drinking their sodas. His son was getting really good it, he thought. Howard was so proud of him that he couldn't give him enough high-fives.

When the kids were all in bed and it was just him and Linda, they sat in the bathroom with the door shut and made love. It wasn't as sexy as he'd thought it would be. The floor was hard and cold, and he kept knocking his head on the commode while he was doing his business. Someday, he thought afterwards, they'd get them a round bed and have some fun with that.

Howard was mellow, and he thought about all the things he was going to do with the money. Mostly he was going to have some fun. He and Linda had even talked about taking the kids to a big park and enjoying the ocean. Neither of them had ever seen it, and he thought that would be a good thing. Yes, sir, he thought, things were finally going their way.

Chapter 9

Hailey wanted to scream and laugh at the same time. She was a freak of nature, she thought, and tried to concentrate on what Dane was teaching her. Today it was mind reading. It wasn't that bad, but it was something that she had to concentrate on so that she'd not let the other person know what she was about.

"Most people, in my experience, only think that they're having a sense of *déjà* vu. As you sift through their memories, you sort of let them see what you are. There are a few that know that you're doing it, but that's not often." She asked her what she did about those people. "I just get what I want and keep moving on. If it's nasty shit—like, I don't know, porn on their computers or something—I suggest to them that they need to stop that shit. That only works if the person is of low intelligence. This family, it won't work on."

Hailey understood that. All the Stantons were super smart. She had two PhDs, so she supposed that put her on their level. But she'd had an extra bit of help by being able to remember everything that she read, while they'd worked hard at their educations.

The only people that knew about that was Colton and her dad. She didn't want them to think any less of her because of what she'd done. When she looked at Dane, she could only imagine what this woman would say about it.

"I'd say that you should use what you have to the betterment of yourself. And when you're reading someone's mind, you'll see that most people would kill to have the kind of memory that you have." Hailey asked her not to read her mind. "I didn't have to. It was written all over your face. If you think for one minute that the Stantons think less of you because of this thing you were born with, then you don't know them very well. They love you for what you bring to them in loving their son. They wouldn't care if you were working for a mobster and killing people for him."

"You did that." Dane told her that she still did it. "And Brayden doesn't care that when you leave your home, you're going to murder someone?"

"He does, but when I leave here to kill, it's because the person is so corrupt and so heinous that murdering him isn't so much that as it is ridding the world of a monster." Hailey told her that she could see that too. "Good. This is what I want you to do. Reach out, well beyond the people here and see if you can find someone. I'd go with someone that you know but be gentle. We don't want them to know that you can do this."

The only person that she felt comfortable with enough to do that to was Ray. She'd been meaning to call her for the last few days, and had been too busy to get to it. Then last night she'd gotten an email from her telling her that she'd put some money in the bank for her to use for David. Nothing more, just that. Hailey figured that Ray was just as busy.

She connected right with her mind, and was surprised to find that she was in a great deal of pain. Telling Dane what she'd discovered, she asked her if she could see what had happened. It was there, on the forefront of her mind.

"Her father is causing some trouble for her. She's sick with worry, too, that he'll find out where David is and come for him." Digging a little deeper, Hailey wanted to go to her right then and give her a hug. "She's lonely while she's in a room full of people. Ray feels like she's failed her grandmother somehow by not making things better for her. She wishes that she could have, by having her and David move in with her."

"Good. Now I want you to just concentrate on her pain. Not just how she got hurt, but what is wrong. Like has she had an accident." Hailey said it was her dad. "Yes, but what did he do to her? You should be able to figure that out as well."

Hailey found the memory of Ray's father and followed that thread. It wasn't hard; he was always on her mind for one thing or another. This time he'd hurt her enough that she'd been hospitalized for several days.

"Her arm is broken. It'll heal, but it hurts because she won't take the medication that the doctor told her to. A deadline is coming up, and she's worried that it won't go the way she wants." Dane told her to gently suggest that she go home and take something, just for one night. "She's thinking about it now. I've told her that she'll be more focused if she has a good night's sleep."

Reading more into her mind, she could see what had happened to her. What, she knew, Ray's father had done. Relaying the information to Dane, Hailey thought if she were there with her, he'd be dead right now.

119

"Tell me what you sense around her. What is she thinking with? Does she have a pencil in her hand? Is she sipping water?" Hailey moved through that and saw something about the room she was in. "What do you mean, you can see the room?"

"Just that. I can see that she has art on the wall that is sort of beautiful, in an abstract sort of way. She has her door open, and there are several employees right outside her office that she likes but doesn't confide in. In her office again, I can see that she has an oak desk that was her grandmother's, and the window is lined with plants. Again, from her grandma. Ray can cook, but she has little time for it much anymore."

Looking at Dane, she had a feeling that she'd done something wrong. Dane had gone with her when they'd been walking through the minds of people around them. Hailey figured that she'd done something wrong in looking around the office.

"You can see what she sees." Nodding, Hailey asked her if she'd done something wrong in that. "No. But I can't do that. I can see their thoughts and memories, and sometimes even unblock some that have been suppressed. But you can actually see what she sees from her point of view."

"You can't do that." Dane shook her head and smiled. It wasn't a friendly one either, but the kind that sort of made Hailey want to run and hide. "What does that mean? I mean, that I can do something you can't. Because as cool as it is to be better at you on something, this is freaking me the fuck out."

"It shouldn't. You have an advantage over me. And while I'm jealous of it, I'd never begrudge you having a power over me." Hailey told her that she would too. "All right, you're right. I'd be crowing like a rooster at sun rise that I could do it. But this is good. I mean, if you can reach out to someone that

I'm assuming is far away, you can see if they're alone, if they have a weapon, and if they were leaving the state in a car or something. This will be epic, Hailey, and save so many lives at the same time."

Hailey asked that they do something else for a while so she could try to wrap her own mind around what she'd figured out. It was creepy, really, to know that she was seeing something that she shouldn't. As they were working on her holding a fireball in her hand, another creepy thing she could do, Lucy and Denny pulled into the yard where they were working.

"I see two of my favorite girls are working out." Lucy kissed them both on the cheek, and Hailey didn't know what to do. "We were going to see if you two would like to come over for some dinner tonight. I know that Colton is out working and won't be back until tomorrow, and Brayden is on an equally long trip for the company that he's thinking of purchasing. My goodness, the boys are certainly busy, aren't they?"

"I'm game—how about you, Hailey?" She didn't know and said that. Dane had become a good friend over the last few weeks, but Hailey was still having trouble being with the entire family. They made her want to curse and beat the shit out of them at the same time. They were just too much for her. "You can even knock me around if you think you can."

Without thinking about what she was doing, Hailey turned to Dane and touched her finger to her forehead. She'd only meant to push her back a little, but the connection was powerful, and she closed her eyes to what she was seeing.

Backing away from Dane when it became too much, they both fell to the ground. Denny was trying to help her while Lucy did the same for Dane. It was as if she'd been drained or something. Hailey backed away from his touch, asking him to wait until she figured this out.

"What the bloody fuck was that?" She shook her head at Dane's question. "I mean it, Hailey, I don't know what you did. Are you hurt from it?"

"I saw it all." Dane stilled and watched her. "The man that you're trying to find is dead. I mean the one working for you, he's dead. He was killed two months ago when he was walked in on while he was copying paperwork from a man's office. The office belongs to a man by the name of Sams. He wasn't supposed to be in there, I'm guessing. However, I'm not sure if the office owner, Sams, is a first name or last."

"Last. His first is Walter. Did he kill him or have someone kill him?" Hailey told her neither. "Then can you tell me who did kill him? He was working undercover for me and Walter Sams. And I'd very much like to figure this out to tell his family where he is."

"He was killed by a man named Stricker. I'm not sure of his first name at all, that's all your boy knew him as." Hailey suddenly felt sick to her stomach, and leaned over to puke twice before she thought that she could stand up. "His body isn't recoverable. He was pushed into a woodchipper while he was still alive."

"Mother fuck. That's some scary yet helpful shit you've got going on there. And I have to tell you again, I didn't feel any of it. Just the power of something rolling over me." Hailey told her that she could have it if she wanted it. "I'm sorry. I'm sorry every day that I did this to you, Hail. I just wanted you to be able to have full use of your hand."

"Well, I certainly got that, didn't I?" She laughed then and sat down on the ground again. "This thing. I can find people that are connected to those who are connected to others. That's fucked up—you know that, don't you?"

Lucy cleared her throat, and Hailey looked up at her when she spoke. "I know that you have been—how do I say?—energized, but I'm sure that there isn't a reason for you two to curse like someone that has been brought up in a brothel, is there?"

"Yes. If you'd let me touch your forehead I'm pretty sure that I can energize you too." Both Lucy and Denny backed away from her. "I'm not going to do that. Once is enough for me."

"What did it feel like? I mean, you were only touching me for seconds—how did you find the connection that quickly?" Hailey was trying to think how to explain it to Dane when she realized that she was feeling hazy, like there was more to something that she had yet to discover about this new power. "Hailey are you all right?"

"I think that's what made me sick. Seeing all that in fast motion like that was like watching a flick in super-fast speed. It was all there, voices, as well as names and places that popped into my head." Hailey thought about all that she'd seen, and laid there while she sorted through it all. "I have a filing cabinet in my mind. I've held my information like that ever since I figured out that everything I read was there. I have a lot of cabinets, as you can imagine. They're marked with things like books I've read, the sound that a bird makes when in a tree. Their names are there, as well as anything that is written about them. I have them for smells, voices, as well as manuals for things that have been outdated. Whatever I could read, smell, or touch, I remember it."

"You have an eidetic memory." She nodded at Denny when he spoke to no one in particular. "Have you always had it? From birth?"

123

"Yes. It's one of the many reasons that my mother hated having me around. When someone gave her a bill or a set of rules that she was to follow, calendar dates and the importance of them were filed away. She didn't like that I knew so much more about things than she ever would." Denny nodded and sat down on the ground close to where she was lying. "I used it to get a good education. I wanted, at one time, to be a lawyer. But after reading case after case of shit people did, I decided that maybe if I taught grade school, I could make a big difference in a child's life."

"I'm sure that you did. Come now, girls, I don't know about you, but I do believe I could eat my weight in salad right now." Hailey asked Lucy if she'd heard what she'd said about her education. "I heard you. Are you expecting me to turn my back on you because you have this wonderful memory that helps people? I won't. I never will, either. What you have, what you've been blessed with, is something that you were meant to have when you came to this family. If you never have another round like you did with Dane just now, it was—well, perfect. To have a family know now that they can mourn for a man that they loved instead of waiting for him to walk through the door."

Hailey looked at Dane, who winked at her. When they were all standing again, Denny held her arm so that she could be steady on her feet. She didn't need it, even told him so, but he said that he needed the contact more than he thought she needed him. Hailey didn't mention again that she was all right now.

~*~

Linda was both excited and nervous about talking to the man that lived there. If he wasn't Hailey's husband, then maybe

124

he'd be able to tell her where she was. They were starving again—the store that she'd been in the first time had figured out what she'd done. They told her not to come back or they'd press charges. And Howie had had the same thing told to him. Bastards. Didn't they know that people had to eat?

Linda straightened herself up and made sure that her hair wasn't too mussy and knocked on the door. Whatever she had expected, it wasn't a large man asking her if he could please help her. They had a butler? Shit fire, that meant that her husband would be able to fork over more cash to get his little wife back. The man cleared his throat and asked her again.

"Yes, I'm wondering if the lady of the house is home. I'm Linda Damon—my daughter is Hailey Whitehead. Is she home?" The butler, or whatever he was, just turned his nose up at her, like she stank or something. "Look, buddy. I want you to tell my daughter to get her ass here this minute. She and I have shit to discuss."

"Mrs. Stanton doesn't reside at this residence. This is the home of Wyatt Stanton. I'm afraid that you're going to be looking for her for some time." She asked him, trying to be polite, where Hailey lived. "No, I don't think so. You can't possibly think that I'm going to tell you that information, miss. The Stantons take pride in having their lives private. I would have thought you'd have figured that out when you couldn't find any personal information about them."

"I want to talk to her. Either you help me, or I'm going to go to every Stanton house and business that I can find and bother all of them. What do you think your all-powerful Stantons will think of you making the mother of one of their wives have to walk all over town to see her? I'm her fucking mother." He didn't so much as blink at her, but stared at her like she had

125

spoiled his suit somehow by simply being near him. "Where is she?"

"I'm afraid that you've set yourself a monumental task then. I shouldn't like to take away from your exercise. I'm sure that someone like you could use a good walk daily." He pulled the door open wider and Linda thought that he was going to let her in. But all he did was show her that he was armed. "Now, be on your way. And good luck with trying to find Mrs. Stanton by going door to door."

The door wasn't slammed in her face but closed quietly, like there was a sleeping child nearby that he didn't want to wake. Linda thought that it was meaner than him slamming the fucking door. Pounding on the door again, she hoped that if there were kids in the house that they'd be just as bratty as hers. Leaving the porch, she walked to the end of the long fucking drive, cursing the entire way.

"What did he mean, someone like me?" Linda looked down at her body and could see that she had put on a few pounds. However, that wasn't any reason for him talking to her like that. She took off her shoes, hating the way the heels that she had were painful to wear.

Before having kids had stretched out her body to mammoth size, she had worn not just high heels, but also skimpy little dresses and pretty things around her throat. But then she'd married Peter and gotten pregnant on the first try, she thought. And her son, Pete, had been like giving birth to a fucking watermelon, and she vowed never to get that way again.

Then she started finding new and more fun men around. They loved her body. Linda had worked really hard at getting her weight back down, and the flab, as she called it, off. Then not too long after she made her spectacular appearance to the world again, she was fucking knocked up, again.

"You'd think that after eight years I might have remembered what to do about having someone's kid." That was when she'd had Hailey. And Peter had been over the moon with her. Even Pete, her big brother, had doted on her like she was a queen. Divorcing Peter had been both a blessing and a curse after that birth.

Linda had only taken Hailey because Peter had loved her more than he did her. Not that she loved him—she wasn't even sure that she ever had. But falling in love with Howie had given her more than she'd ever gotten in the relationship with Peter. Then Hailey had grown up.

Standing at the driveway to the house of the next Stanton that she'd found an address for, she wasn't sure what to do. There was a man in the guard house that didn't make her think of one of those fat wanna be cops like she'd seen on television. This guy was sharply dressed, and looked like he'd kill you for farting in his direction.

He came out of the little house, and she realized that he was bigger than she'd first thought. The man was as big as the bears she'd seen at the circus one time when they'd taken the kids. Seeing him coming toward her, Linda felt like she should turn and run when he was standing in front of her.

"Do you need something?" Linda nodded, completely forgetting what she was there for. The man's voice sounded like he was only one roar away from having her as a tasty snack. "Well, what is it?"

"You're very rude. Does your employer know how you talk to guests? I've been invited here." Linda thought the idea was brilliant and smiled at the man as she continued. "My daughter lives here, and she's invited me to have lunch with her. I forgot the code to the gate, so if you could open it for me, I'll be on my way."

"What's your daughter's name? And so you know, I know you're lying through your teeth. What's her name?" Before she could think that the man was really getting nasty with her, she barked out Hailey's name like she'd been on a three-day drunk and was puking up her guts. "Miss Hailey doesn't live here. Miss Dane does. And if you're as smart as you seem to think you are, then you'd not want to tangle with her either."

"What do you mean, either? Are you trying to tell me that this Dane person would try and harm me?" The bear, because he was reminding her more and more of one, just smiled and shook his head. "Then why is it you sounded as if you were threatening me with her for some reason?"

"Miss Dane doesn't suffer fools well. And she won't harm you. You fuck with her and you will be dead. She doesn't like to do things the second time, and you've made a nuisance of yourself enough today as far as the Stantons are concerned." Linda's temper, not very stable anyway, seemed to rocket out of her and she aimed it at the man. But before she could so much as lift her hand to slap him, he continued. "You fuck with me and they'll never find your body. On that, you can go to the bank."

She saw it then, the shifting of man to bear along his skin. And when she backed away, nearly tripping twice on her sore bare feet, he laughed. It was hearty, like she'd heard the Santas in the mall do. But this was dangerous, and he wasn't going to be handing out candy canes when she left.

Turning away from him, she heard the man shout her name. He knew her name? She turned to see what he could want, but when he told her to leave town or else, she had a feeling that she needed to go back to the hotel right now and pack her family and be gone. Maybe even leave them there to face this man while she made good on her escape.

Linda decided to not bother with seeing the others about Hailey. Two more of the large homes were right on her path back to the car, but she didn't even bother looking up the long drives. This shit had just gotten real, and she was as afraid as she'd ever been.

Walking toward the hotel, Linda thought about the encounters that she'd had. Yes, the men had been rude to her, but she figured that they were because of something that Hailey had told them. Not that she believed Hailey would lie about anything she'd done to them, but that still didn't make it right that she wasn't getting to see her.

"Damn it all to fuck and back." When she was going through the little town, so small that it didn't even have a movie theater, she saw a woman standing by her car. Linda had left it there so that it would not make its loud noises around the Stantons' homes. She had been sure that it would make her look more like the white trash that the people already thought she was. When she got closer to the car, she was ready to tell the woman to fuck off when she smiled.

"Hailey?" The woman nodded but didn't speak yet. "I've been all over this fucking town looking for your ass. Where have you been hiding?"

"I wasn't hiding, Linda. But at home, enjoying my time with my dad and husband. Oh, Dad asked me to tell you something. He said to tell you that he knows that I'm not his daughter, but he loves me despite you being a whore." She told her not to call her by her first name, that she was still her mother. "You might have given birth to me, Linda, but you were never a mother.

Maybe a mother fucker, but not a loving mother. What is it you hope to gain by coming here and stalking me?"

"I want some money." Hailey nodded, and Linda let out a breath that she'd been holding for what seemed like days and days. "I want you to start paying us a monthly amount too. Or I go to that new husband of yours and tell him what sort of person you really are."

"I've told him that you sold me off to men five times my age. I've even told him about how high my IQ is. He doesn't care about that, but loves that, unlike you when you speak, I can have an intelligent conversation with him. And if you really think that I'm going to pay you once more, you're insane. And you can fucking forget about any payments that you want too. I told you, I'm done with your fucking ass, and want you to leave me the fuck alone."

"Does he know your part in the Nelson shit? I bet he doesn't know as much as I do. I should tell him what you really did for those people." Hailey just leaned against the car and said nothing. "I want you to pay me what you owe me."

"Owe you? What on earth can you think that I'd owe you for? I made my own way through high school and college. I paid for my home, the car that I had, as well as anything I wanted. What could I possibly owe to you, Linda? Maybe you're mistaking the money that *you* owe *me*. I'd like for you to pay me back, but we both know that you have nothing, and have resorted to stealing food instead of finding a job and working for what you need."

"That's a lie. You owed me that money, too." Hailey said nothing, but looked over Linda's shoulder at someone behind her. Linda turned to see a very well dressed and gorgeous man there, and wondered what the fuck he could want. "What the fuck are you doing? Taking a survey? Get your ass away from us. I'm talking to my daughter."

"I'm her husband." He moved around her to wrap his arm around Hailey. Christ, she'd bagged herself one with money and good looks. "Are you still drugging your kids at night when you go out and try to break into houses? That shit is going to get you in major trouble if you keep it up. Maybe you should heed what you were told and get the hell out of our town."

"What, the big bad man is going to yell at me more? Who exactly wears the pants in your family? Is it you or my daughter?" He told her that they were interchangeable depending on the idiot they were talking to. "Are you calling me an idiot? You fucking bastard."

When she drew back her hand to slap the man, Hailey stood in front of him. She wondered if it was a joke, a woman protecting a man. But no, Linda could see it in her eyes. Hailey would indeed kill her if she so much as touched her husband.

Linda was overwhelmed then. They had knowledge about her that could and would get her into some serious shit. Looking at Hailey, she knew that her giving them any money, even enough for a newspaper, was a dead end. Whatever they knew about her and Howie was going to get them taken to prison. If not, jail time for sure. However they'd heard about whatever they had on her, Linda knew it was going to be a death warrant for her and Howie.

Turning on her bare feet again, she left them standing there. The laughter behind her pissed her off, but she didn't turn back. It was time to roll up the sidewalk on this journey. They were beating a dead horse in getting anything from her daughter. Linda was afraid for the first time since she'd walked out on her first husband.

Her and Howie, they were going to be arrested soon, Linda thought, if not today, then very soon. When she got to the hotel, forgetting about the car, she had to sit down or pass out. It took her nearly an hour to feel calm enough to tell Howie what had happened. Christ, they were in deeper shit than they'd ever been since being together.

Chapter 10

Hailey was very quiet when they got home. Colton had left her to herself out on the deck when she'd asked him to. She'd stood up to her tormentors and had come out on top. But that didn't mean that she wasn't heartbroken by the verbal abuse from her mother had done to her. Colton sat in the living room with his mom and dad. They too were hurting because Hailey was.

"I want to go out there and kick that woman's ass." Both he and Dad looked at Mom, shocked. "I've been hanging around Dane and Hailey a lot lately. I think they're rubbing off on me. Perhaps I should go talk to Allie and Tess for a few days. Though I don't think they're any less of a bad influence on me."

"I'd not call it bad, but just you saying what you felt. Thank you." They all turned to Hailey when she spoke. Colton went to her, unsure how to bring up the subject of Linda, so he decided to wait on her lead. Every time he encountered things like this with her, all his training to be someone that should know what to do went out the door. "I'm sorry, but I needed a few minutes to come to terms with something that only just occurred to me coming home. I don't love my mother. And other than my childhood when I was little, I don't think I ever did. And it broke my heart. Not for me, but for her. She's a sad woman, and I'm finished with her and Howard."

"That's good news. I have to tell you something, something that as a doctor bothers me a great deal. I have a buddy that works in Columbus, and he told me that just before they got to town, he thought that they'd purchased a lot of drugs from him that were used as sleep aids. At the time he didn't think anything about it. They weren't high when he saw them. And after talking with Colton last night, I'm thinking that they've been giving it to those kids so that they'll sleep a lot." She asked him just how sure he was that they'd bought it. "I showed him a picture. I occasionally show him some that I'm concerned with. The two of us, we get together at times to compare notes, so to speak. And he went through his phone and found them. Ben, he sells it on the street and then busts the people that bought it. He'd not realized that the Damons were in transit, on their way here, so now he knows."

"And what is he going to do with that information? Do you know, Dad?" His dad nodded, and Colton sat down, pulling Hailey onto his lap. "I have a feeling that this is going to be epic."

"Not so much." Hailey asked him why not. "I told him what was going on here and that we were dealing with something else altogether. I explained to him that my newest daughter-in-law needed closure. You do, don't you, honey? Telling us how you feel about them is good, but I think you need to end your relationship by confronting them."

"But the children? As much as I dislike them, I don't want

anything to happen to them. We can't just leave them there." Dad looked at Mom and Hailey did too. "Why do I think you have as many contacts as even Dane has, if not more? But yours are less unscrupulous."

"Yes, well, a mother does what she needs to do to keep her children safe and not worrying. I called Child Services just the other day. They sent a van out to get the children, but they didn't answer the door. They have to have a reason for busting in, apparently. Stupid rule if you ask me, when there are little ones involved. With what Denny found out, there will be some door busting, but when the parents aren't there. There're going to be bigger fish to fry, I think."

Colton asked his dad if they had everything set up. Taking children from their parents was something that medical personnel tried very hard to avoid. But in this case, it was necessary. They could kill their own children with what they were doing. His dad said that he'd been hoping that he'd take care of it.

They'd have to have the poison taken out of their bodies. If what Dad thought was true, these kids might have become dependent on the drugs. And on kids, no matter the age, it would hurt them most of all if their bodies weren't in good shape health wise. Colton didn't think that any of them were, but he'd take this one step at a time. He had had contact with the children, and even then they were malnourished and dehydrated. The situation hadn't gotten any better, he didn't think.

After his parents left them, Colton asked if Hailey wanted to come into his office while he made arrangements. He kept a close eye on her as he made the calls necessary to make sure that the children were all right. There were specific families that were specially trained to deal with children who might be hooked on some kind of drug.

"Are you all right?" She nodded at him and smiled. It was genuine, he thought—she really was all right. "This is going to rip this family apart. Not that it wasn't going to happen anyway, but there is too much going on in all their lives right now to think that anyone won't come out battered and bruised."

"I've been thinking on that as well. I don't know if I have it in me to take on my half family." He asked her what she meant. "Just that. They're beyond control that I'd know how to deal with. They've been brought up feeling that they're privileged, that someone else is to blame for what is going wrong in their lives. The little time that I spent with them when I was dealing with my parents, they were destructive, mouthy, and nasty to everyone. I can't think that they'd be any different, no matter what I did, because I believe that they'd blame me for their parents not being with them."

"You think this or do you know? I heard what happened between you and Dane today. So I can imagine that you've been able to peer right into all of their minds without any trouble. So, again, do you think this or do you know?" She seemed hesitant in answering him, so he waited. Hailey wasn't one to say something that she couldn't back up. "If you'd like my opinion on them, I'd say that you're right. They not only would blame you for their woes, but maybe be dangerous to you if given the chance."

"They would. And they have been." She wandered around the room not touching anything, just wandering around. "Once when Linda asked to *borrow* money, I went to their house. It was government housing that had recently been built. But you'd never think that it was only a few months old to have

136

seen it. Anyway. Linda had me come directly to her house. She either didn't have a car or it didn't run. So I went there."

Colton was almost afraid to ask what they'd done to her, because as surely as he was sitting there, he knew that one or all of them had done something. When she sat on the couch that had only just arrived today, she was fluffing the pillows when she continued.

"The kids were in the back yard. They weren't playing like I had assumed they were, but were hurting a small dog, to the point where they were just dragging his poor little body around on a rope that had been tied around its neck." Hailey put the pillow down and picked up the other one. "I went out to rescue the poor thing, wondering why Linda hadn't seen what they were doing. As soon as I walked out to them, the oldest one threw a rock at me and hit me in the head. It was bleeding pretty steadily when I stood up after it knocked me on my ass. One of the others, I don't know which, hit me in the stomach with a ball bat. And you want to know the most horrific part of it was? Linda stood on the back porch, and was laughing at what they were doing to me."

"Come here, love." He didn't think she was going to, but would just sit there as she finished her tale. Colton knew that something else had happened that day, but it was up to her to tell him what had happened. "Come here and sit with me so that I don't shift and find the lot of them and kill them all."

Hailey sat down on him. She spoke softly to him, her voice void of any kind of emotion. Her family, because he was sure that was what she'd considered them to be until that point, had hurt her both mentally and physically.

"The neighbor called the police and an ambulance for me. By that time, I'd lost consciousness. By the time they got there for me, Linda and her kids had left. Hiding out, no doubt." She turned on his lap, facing him, with her legs on either side of his. "I'd left my purse there. The cash that I'd been asked for, the ten grand that she owes me, was gone, as were my credit cards, when I got it back. They couldn't use the cards, because I have it set up that there has to be identification shown before it can be accepted for use. And I was the only one that had a card. But the money, she took it, or her kids did. Make love to me, Colton. I want you to wash it all away now that I've told you."

When she kissed him, her hands all over his body taking his shirt off, Colton stopped her by holding her hands in front of him. She was rough, which he could understand, and he wasn't sure that she wanted him to wash it all away or to take her anger out on him. Hailey looked at him when he said her name.

"Who am I?" She told him his name. "That's my name, but I want you to tell me who I am. Am I your mother, Linda? Your half siblings? Or perhaps Howard."

"They took away every bit of my trust and hurt me with it." Colton nodded, waiting on her to answer him. When she took in a deep breath and started sobbing, Colton held her to him as he would have a small child. "It wasn't the only time that they hurt me. Even when I'd make my...Linda meet me someplace public, it was the same thing. If it wasn't her kids it was her. Once she put her hand onto mine and sliced my hand up with a razor she had there. It happened after I told her that there wasn't going to be any more money. Of course, I gave it to her so that I'd be able to have my hand back. After that, I didn't even bother with going to give it to her. It was safer and easier to just send it to someplace as a wire transfer."

Hailey hadn't had a good life. The only time, he'd bet, that she'd had anything resembling a safe home was living with her father in the comfortable home that she'd provided for him. And that had been taken away from her too.

Colton held her until she stopped crying. Realizing that she'd fallen asleep, he picked her up in his arms and took her to their room. Laying her down and pulling a light blanket over her, Colton kissed her gently on the forehead before leaving her. It was time that Colton took care of his wife.

The first thing he did was talk to his dad, telling him that he wanted them there when the children were taken. After telling him what Hailey had gone through, he said he'd have it done now.

But don't involve the adults. They're mine. His dad, a reasonable man who took his Hippocratic oath seriously, asked him if he could go with him to end their miserable fucking lives. Both his parents had cursed in one day, and he was beginning to think that they were as bad as the rest of them. They only chose to curse when necessary. And this, he thought, was very necessary. *I have to think about what to do. I need to have all my ducks in a row before I confront them. Because as surely as I am in love with Hailey, I want them to be aware of every single one of their crimes against her.*

The first thing that he did was start a list. He wrote down everything that Hailey had told him, the things that he knew and what he'd heard. Asking Dane to dig all of it up for him had her asking if she could be there as well. She had a bone to pick with them too.

In fact, my dear brother, I think that every one of us would like to take their piece. You can even count on your parents to want a part in this. Colton laughed and said that when he was finished with his to do list, he'd bring it before them all. *You give me an hour. I'll have more than you thought possible on them.*

139

Colton was afraid that Dane was correct in that. That they were only scratching the surface on these people. As he began his list of shit that was going to rain down on them, he found himself smiling. They were going to pay, by God.

Chapter 11

Howie was certain that they'd walked two hundred miles today. They'd had to stretch out their shopping now that they'd been caught at the first store. But while his feet were tired, and his body ached, they'd gotten enough stuff to last them a few more days. He had no idea why, but shopping like this gave him a bigger thrill than he'd ever experienced before.

"How much longer are we going to be here? I'm telling you, Howie, there was something very scary about them. Including Hailey's husband. She wasn't the least bit afraid of me, nor did she seem to care one whit that we needed her to pay us. I think we should cut our losses and figure out a way to get back home. We might live longer, I'm thinking." He just looked at her. "You didn't see her face when she was talking to me. It scared the shit out of me, if you want to know the truth."

"We're not leaving. I don't know how you think it would be possible for us to leave town when your daughter hasn't given us any funds to make it happen." Linda said that she didn't think she would, either. "You'll see. Once we have her where we want her, that husband of hers will pay up to get her back. And I think for our troubles, you should get the first crack at making her sorry for making us get to that point."

He had to think sometimes to remember why they thought that she should be paying them. There had been the blackmailing thing, but that had gone to bust. But before they'd even known about all that, they'd been taking what they could from her. When he remembered it, he smiled to himself as he thought of the look on her face when she'd been told what to do.

Howie thought his kids were a nuisance, and they drove him crazy most of the time. But when the chips were down, which was nearly all the time, they would come through for them. Why, just before they left home, his oldest—and the one he was most proud of—had gone into a store and come back out with over five hundred dollars in cash. Howie had read in the paper how some hooligan had robbed the store where his son had been. But Howie didn't care—the money had been the best, because they'd celebrated for two days with it.

Of course they were broke again, but again and again their son had helped them out. The younger ones could shop better than he could. Howie thought it was their smile that got them out of trouble. Even as bad as they were, they could charm the shit out of someone when necessary.

But the first time that he'd had Linda approach Hailey was the beginning of a wonderful relationship. And now that was fucking being messed with because Hailey wanted to show off to her new husband.

Hailey had been called to them when Linda had had an accident. She'd not had one really, but it brought Hailey home, and Linda had nearly messed it up when Hailey said that she wasn't paying for any medications since they were on a medical card from the state.

It took him taking over to get her to give them some money. He'd told her how the kids didn't have any winter coats, nor did they have any of their school supplies. Relenting then, she'd given them enough money to pay for coats for the kids, and also one for Linda and Howie. Plus, she'd added in what Howie had told her the fees at school and supplies cost.

Two grand they got from her. Two grand that they'd used for other things that they thought were more important.

The government gave his kids coats every year, even some for himself and Linda. And the school gave them all their supplies, as well free lunches. Howie had no idea why people even had jobs when the government provided everything that they needed—even Christmas presents that they'd sell and pocket the money for.

He'd trained them on how to get things to bring home, too. A carton or two of milk, some sandwiches that were only a little smashed, as well as fruit. He hadn't cared all that much for apples and such, but they filled his belly better than nothing did.

But it had gotten harder and harder to get Hailey to help them out. He had no idea why she didn't want to have her little brothers and sister have more, but she'd gotten stubborn about it, and they'd had to reduce themselves to violence.

Not that he didn't like knocking her around some. She wasn't very smart, he'd always figured, and said to Linda that she'd not graduated from any place, much less college, but had quit school and was getting her money by prostitution. Hell, he thought, they'd broken her into that sort of income. Howie didn't know why she'd begrudge them a little green once in a while.

And now this shit. Who did she think she was, handing over money right and left then taking it away? They had gotten used to her helping them out, and when she'd cut them off, he thought to call the police on her or something. There had to be a law or something that would make her keep up with giving them some cash.

By the time they got back to the hotel room, he'd thought of five plans to get Hailey and had dismissed them all. Now that she had a husband around, knocking her around wouldn't get them far. Besides, Howie was sure that he held the purse strings, so to speak, and they'd have to get around to him for help.

The food went a long way when the kids were sleeping. He knew that he should feel bad about keeping his kids on drugs, but sometimes the noise was just too much. And they were forever whining about how hungry they were, how they wanted to go into the yard and play.

There was nothing like a yard there, just a parking lot, but they couldn't go out until Hailey paid up. He told them that too, that all this was her fault and that they needed to pin the blame right where it belonged.

Linda hid all the things that they liked the best. Otherwise the kids would get into them before they could. Howie was looking forward to having a nice hot meal for a change, and his mouth nearly watered when Linda brought out the chocolate covered cherries for them both to eat while the kids were out.

The door exploded open just as they were opening the second box of the treat, and the four men that came into the room were heavily armed, so he did just what they told him. Getting down on his knees with his hands over his head, it occurred to him that there might be some kind of drug bust or something going on next door. The police were just making sure that they'd not been in on it.

When he tried to explain to them that they were just a family on vacation, there wasn't any need for them to do this, one of the fuckers popped him in the mouth with his gun. After that, he was tossed to the floor and a booted foot was pressed hard against his shoulders.

"What is the meaning of this? You can't just break into someone's room and treat them like this." The man that had hit him in the face told him to shut the fuck up before he put a bullet in his fucking head. "I'm going to report this to your bosses, see if I don't. And I'm going to be getting your checks every month, as well as your pension."

Howie shut his mouth when the man pressed even harder on his shoulders—it was getting difficult to breathe. So, when his hands were jerked up behind him and cuffed, someone rolled him over and Howie took a needed deep breath.

A woman came in a few minutes later. Boot guy told her it was all clear and that she could proceed. He watched in horror as a doctor, he assumed that was what he was, told the medics with him to take the children out. Linda was screaming at the cops to let her up, but Howie was more worried about his kids with a doctor.

They were going to be screwed if they did any sort of blood tests on the children. They had been giving them something since birth, he thought. And it had never hurt them, so why stop, he told himself. But now the police were involved, and he was afraid of what they'd do to the two of them.

The woman knelt down to where he was lying and smiled at him. It was far from friendly, so he kept his mouth shut. He was at a disadvantage right his minute, or he thought that he would gladly kick her ass. She looked over at Linda when she continued to scream at them to let her go.

"You're in so much deep shit that I wonder if you'll ever get to see sunlight again before I'm finished with you." Howie asked her what the hell she was talking about. "For starters, I'm betting that your kids are going to need some major hospital time to wean them off of the fucking drugs that you've had them on, at least since you've been here."

"I have no idea what you're talking about. And I would appreciate it if you were to show me a warrant for busting into a room that has nothing to do with you." She slapped some papers on his chest as she laughed. "This means nothing to me. You've taken my kids. I think that someone could call that kidnapping."

"You'd think that, wouldn't you?" She looked over at Linda and yelled at her. "Shut the fuck up before I have to come over there and shut you up myself. I have had it up to my ass with you two, and your screaming about your precious babies isn't helping anyone."

Linda's mouth, like his earlier, snapped closed. Howie wanted to comfort her, but at the moment, he was hogtied and at their mercy. But it wouldn't always be like this. He'd have the upper hand and this bitch's badge for what she'd done to him today.

"I don't wear a badge. I'm here in case you get sassy with them, and to take you out if you do. Sad, really, that you've been keeping that lying fucking tongue behind your teeth. I was looking forward to blowing your fucking head off before I start on your wife." He believed her. Howie had a feeling that she would pull out a gun and shoot him even with all the police around. "You can take that to the bank, fucktard."

He realized then that he'd not spoken aloud. The woman had read his mind, and when she laughed, the sound of it like nails being run over a chalkboard, he felt his ass pucker up and his balls curl up tighter to his body. When she stood up, he let out a breath that he'd been holding, not sure what was going on. But Howie thought that for now he was safe. Then she touched her hand to his face.

He didn't even have it in him to scream at the pain. Howie felt as if his head had exploded, that she'd somehow ripped out his brain through his mouth. Whatever she was doing, he was in a great deal of pain, and he knew somehow that he'd never be the same when she finished. If he wasn't dead from this.

Images of his life, from his childhood until the theft at the store, ran through his head like it was going to come out of his eyes and would be displayed on the wall for all to see. The things that he'd done to Hailey, his own kids, and even his own parents. Memory after memory shifted around until it was in order, like his life was ticking backwards and he had a front row seat to it all. When she let go of him, the whatever it was didn't finish. He had lived a horrific life, and it had all been things he'd done to others.

Lying there, limp, he watched her with no movement except his eyes. The rest of him was in too much pain, which was gripping him in every muscle, to turn and see what she was doing now. When he heard Linda screaming, he knew that whatever she'd done to him, she was doing it to his lovely wife too.

Howie hurt still when they were left there on the floor. His cuffs had been taken off; the terrible pain from being rolled over to do so had had him screaming again. And when the woman came back, standing over him like some kind of avenging angel,

147

she hit him again, and Howie was actually thankful when he passed out.

~*~

Colton couldn't take his eyes off the little boy that was fighting for his life. The dosage of drugs that he'd been given had built up in his body until it could hold it no longer. His breaths were slow and being helped along with a canula. The twitching of his arms and legs was so violent that he'd had to be restrained so he'd not hurt himself. His dad sat down beside him, and Colton, for the first time in his adult life, wanted his dad to hold him while he cried.

"I've talked to the doctors with the children. The little girl passed away about an hour ago—the drugs had taken their toll on her major organs and they simply shut down. Even if we had taken the kids sooner, the outcome would have been the same." Colton knew that too. He'd talked to the doctor that had come in to see about this one. "I'm so sorry, son, I truly am."

"Hailey is with the other boy. His name is Howard too. The doctor said the same thing about him as he did this little boy—his name is James, by the way. It had been a long-term thing, them feeding their own children doses of drugs that would have killed a grown man." His dad was crying softly, but said nothing. "Carlton told me—he's in charge of the emergency room—that if they were to live, which he very much doubts that they will, they will need round the clock care because their minds have been affected as well. Christ, Dad, these are their own fucking children. How could they be so careless like this?"

"I don't know, son. I wish that I did. When I was first working as a doctor, nothing like this was around. And if it was, then you heard very little about it. Even as doctors, we would compare notes on what happened, but we never dreamed that

148

it would come to this. At least I never did."

The monitors over the bed started singing their song of impending death. As they moved out of the way of the nurses and doctors, James was gone before anything could have been done to revive him.

"I'm going to see Hailey. She's taking this hard, and I want to be with her."

"Your mom is with her right now. Come with me, and we'll step outside for a few moments. It'll do you some good. You've not moved from that room since they were brought in two days ago."

He was numb. While Colton didn't know these children, he had heard stories about them that he would never have believed from anyone but Hailey. But their passing was difficult to comprehend because of the way that they'd been taken so young.

Moving out the doors into the night, he was surprised that he hadn't even realized that it was this late. Or early, however you wanted to look at it. Sitting on the bench that was just out of the emergency room, Colton felt like he'd been dragged along a stone path and that he'd hit every rock on the way. Standing up, he stretched, feeling his muscles protest at the movement. Colton sat back down and said nothing for some time. Neither did his dad, as they both seemed to be lost in their thoughts.

"I haven't talked to Hailey about it yet, but I would like to make sure that they're buried properly. I don't even know where to begin on that. Will you help us, Dad?" Dad said that he'd be there for the two of them. "She's going to go see them tomorrow and tell them what has happened. They were still in that hotel room the last time they were checked. They're only there because the agencies that want to take them in aren't all assembled just yet. I wish that they'd do something so that they could be taken out."

"I feel your pain, son. I do. Those people were given a great and wonderful gift, and they murdered it. Those poor little babies. I cannot imagine what they've gone through in their short lives." Colton felt Hailey's profound sorrow and told her to come to him. "Your mother just told me that the other child has passed away as well. Three lives, cut so terribly short by the two people in this world who should have been there for them."

"Hailey is coming to us. She's taking it hard. I think she's feeling a little guilty, too, about the conversation that we had just before this happened. We were discussing what would happen to them, who would take them in." Dad said that him and his mom had spoken about it too. "Had they lived, they would have blamed her for them not being with their parents. And I agreed with her. She told me what they'd done to her in the name of getting money from her. Christ, Dad, those people are monsters."

Hailey came through the doors that they had just exited. She was sobbing, and told him that Howard had passed away too. That she wished that she could have been there for them, done something to keep them safe. Colton said nothing to her — there was nothing she could have done. She'd not been aware of the drugs until they came here. He held her while she cried, and Dad went inside. Taking her to the bench, they both sat there clinging to each other for support.

"I'd like to have them buried, please." Colton told her that he'd thought the same thing, and would do anything for her. "I want to go there right now and tell them what they've done. They no more deserved those children than they did me. Dane said that they had gone grocery stealing, and had left those poor babies all alone. I cannot fathom parents that would do such a thing and think it was not going to turn out just the way it has."

"Me either, honey." He didn't want her to cry. It was tearing him up inside that he couldn't do a thing to help her. Colton felt like he was failing her in some way, not able to make things right for her.

Dane came to join them when Hailey gained a little control over herself. "I would like to ask you a favor, Hailey. Denny just told us all that all three children had passed away. I am profoundly sorry for your loss, but I'd like to find who the mother fucker was that sold them the drugs. I think you can help with that trail thing that you can do." Colton said to Dane that he thought that an undercover cop had sold the drugs to them. "No, the drugs that he's selling are no more than a mixture of sugar and a dose of caffeine to give them a little boost. I've talked to the doctors here that were treating them, and he said that it was high grade heroin. That all three of them had enough in their system to kill someone twice their size and weight."

"What do you want me to do? I'll do anything that you need to make that fucker pay for his crimes." Colton could feel her resolve. He knew that Hailey would do this and feel useful, helpful to the children. "Do you need me to go there and see them? If you do, then I want you to know that they're as good as dead. And they'll suffer for it to the very end."

"Oh, they're going to suffer, all right. When I'm finished with them, they'll wish they'd never been born. Trust me, Hailey, when I tell you that I know ways of hurting someone that would turn your stomach. This was something that I did before." Colton thought that was an understatement, but he wasn't going to tell Hailey that. Instead, he held her hand while Dane told her what she needed to do. "I've touched them both and raped their minds. I wasn't the least bit gentle about it, either. I know the face of the man who is selling them, but I have a feeling that there are more involved in this drug action."

"All right. You do know that it's going to sap us both. I don't want someone coming up on us and seeing you fly through the air." Colton had heard about the incident that had happened the other day. And when Brayden came out of the ER with their brother Wyatt, he stood up when Hailey did. "You're going to be there for her, but I have to warn you, I haven't any idea what I might find or if you'll be hurt with this. All this is new shit for me."

"We understand. Wyatt is here in the event that someone needs medical help. And I'm going to hold onto Dane to make sure that if we both fly through the air when you do this, then I can break her fall." Colton asked what he could do. "I was hoping that if this does affect me in some way, you'll take some of the whatever the fuck this is too. I'm thinking that you should be hurt as badly as I might be."

They were laughing when he stood behind Hailey. All she'd done before was touch her finger to Dane's head. She still talked about how the images that she'd found were so clear in her head that she could retrace Dane's life from the moment she'd been born until then. He only hoped that this would give them what they wanted. One less drug dealer on the streets was fine by him.

Colton wrapped his arms around her waist as Brayden had done for Dane. Wyatt was standing by with a medical kit. There probably wouldn't be any use for it, since they were all four shifters of some kind, but he wanted to make sure that he was there. Colton loved his brother for that.

Hailey inhaled deeply and then let out her breath slowly and easily. When she reached up with just her pointer finger to Dane's head, he braced himself for whatever happened. As soon as Hailey touched her, Colton felt like he'd stuck his wet finger in a light socket and fried every inch of himself.

Colton had no idea what had happened, but Hailey was standing over him shouting his name. Christ, that had hurt, but she didn't look like she'd been touched by the same thing as him. Sitting up, he was dizzy at first, but was able to stand after a few minutes. Wyatt was still cursing as Brayden was helped to his feet as well.

"I don't ever want to be here when you do something like that again. The four of you were bright enough to look like you were a fucking light bulb. And when you guys went backwards, as if you had a pull string on you, I nearly wet my fucking pants when you hit something with the full impact of a fucking truck." Wyatt shook himself and Brayden, laughing, asked him if he was all right. "Fuck you. I thought it would be a simple thing. Just a touch, Dane had told me. Hailey would touch her and that would be it but for the falling down. Hell, guys, I think if you guys had been standing with a wall on either side of you, you would have gone through it."

He did calm down enough to check them both out. They were fine except for the fact that Wyatt had hit Brayden, bloodying his nose when he wouldn't stop laughing at him. When it was assured that they were all fine, Colton asked Hailey if she had it.

"Yes. And you're not going to believe who it is." Dane said a name, and when Hailey nodded, she stood up. "You knew? Then why did you have me do this? To take out our mates?

153

Was that the plan?"

"Nah, that was just a bonus. I thought I knew, but on something like this, I'd have to be sure. When I call the man I'm working for, he's going to take care of the teacher for us." Colton asked her which one. "None other than the sixth-grade science teacher at the elementary school not far from here. I'll take it from here. Anything else that I should know about?"

"Yes, a couple of things, but those can wait for now. But tell Sams that I said for him to watch his back around his nephew. He has a plot in his head that will hurt a great many people if not nipped in the bud." Dane stared at Hailey for a full minute before she nodded and walked to her car with Brayden. "She's going to hate doing this one. The person in question has been teacher of the year five times in a row. I guess now we know why."

He was sitting there on the bench when he realized that she'd left him there. She had just made a joke. It had been so serious and so—well, funny, that he was still laughing about it when he entered the hospital again. But as soon as he realized what he had to do now, he sobered up. This was going to be difficult for a great many people.

Chapter 12

Howie didn't know why no one had come to arrest them. He had it in his head that Hailey had paid them off and now they were free and clear. He missed the kids, but honestly, they'd been a lot to handle. He missed them, but he didn't care that they were gone. Howie asked Linda how she was feeling.

Whatever had happened to them when that woman touched them, it had affected them for hours. Once he'd been able to get up on his own, he'd realized that not only had he pissed himself, but he'd also shit his pants. Luckily, he'd been able to clean himself up before Linda woke up. He didn't want to feel stupid in front of her.

"When do you suppose we'll be able to go and see the kids? I mean, it's been four or five days, hasn't it? And we've not heard anything. And calling the hospital got us nothing. I guess that Hailey took care that we'd not know how well our children are faring." Linda had been so quiet for the last few days, only speaking to ask about the kids, that he was fearful that she'd had her mind messed with.

155

Howie knew that he'd had his mind read. Of course, it had taken him most of yesterday to figure that out. While he was worried about how much she'd gotten, his fear of getting into deep shit lessened every day. When someone knocked on the door, he didn't have any problem opening it. The manager had told them that they were paid up for the rest of the month. When asked if they'd leave before the end if they got the extra money, Howard had just turned his back on the man. Hailey again, he'd bet anything.

The couple standing there, he knew; Hailey—Christ, he was blown away by her beauty every time he saw her—and one of the Stanton men. He had no idea which one, but Linda certainly did. When they asked to come in, Howie opened the door wider and stepped back.

He figured that if he got them inside, he could knock them out and take their cash. Both of them were well dressed. The man had on a black suit that he'd bet cost more then he'd had all month in cash. And Hailey was wearing an equally black dress that seemed sort of somber to him.

"What the fuck do you want? Unless it's to give us money, then you can get back on your high horse and fuck off. You had them take our children away from us. What kind of sick fucking thing is that?" Hailey told Linda that they were dead. "What did you just say to me? Did you just threaten me, Hailey? I hope so, because I'm going to—"

"The children are gone—they passed away two days ago." Linda was still staring at Hailey, but Howie fell to the bed, then slipped to the floor. Dead? His children were dead? How the fuck did that happen? "They died of drug overdoses. The three of them had too much in their systems to combat the issues that they'd had with long term usage. You murdered them by giving them drugs."

"No. You're lying to make me upset. Christ, Hailey, we might have our differences, but I'm your mother and this is beyond cruel of you." Howie still couldn't wrap his mind around the statement. His children were dead. When the newspaper was tossed to him on the floor, it was turned to the obituary page and he read their names and ages like it wasn't them. "Howie? What's going on here? She's lying, isn't she? Please tell me that she's lying. I need to hear you say that to me."

"Their funeral was today — this morning, as a matter of fact. I've taken care that they had a proper funeral and were buried in the cemetery in town. Their headstones won't be put in yet — they're being made right for them." Hailey looked at them both, so much hatred on her face that Howie was sure that she'd burn them with it. "What do you have to say for yourselves? You murdered three little children that had done nothing to you two but had the misfortune of being born to you."

"How could you not tell us that they died until they were buried? How could you do that to us? Our kids are gone, and you're standing there in your fancy dress with your fancy husband telling us that we murdered the kids. What about you? Had you just given us the money, then they'd not have had to be drugged like that." Howie looked over at Linda when she started screaming at Hailey not to lie to her, that her children were fine. Howie looked back at the two of them as he continued. "This is your mother, Hailey. How could you do this to her? This is beyond even what I thought you'd be capable of."

"If I had given you money, then things would have been all right? You were feeding them drugs long before you got here to blackmail me again. Admit it. You murdered them long before you came to see how much more you could get from me." The man wrapped his arms around the waist of Hailey. For some reason that pissed Howard off.

Hailey had support. Someone to take care of her when times were rough. He doubted that she'd ever had a rough time in all her life. And from what Linda had told him and what he remembered, she had never carried her own weight when it came to their household. She was always away doing homework or some shit like that. When he stood up, Howie heard the man growl low and he looked at him when he spoke.

"You touch her and you'll die. Right here on this floor. There will be no funeral for you, no one to mourn your passing. I will make sure that your body is never found, and that you'll rot in hell where you belong." He told him that he had no right to talk to him that way. "Don't I? I've seen what you've been doing all these years. What kinds of things you taught your kids to help you with. You and your wife are monsters, and neither of you deserved to be the parent to anyone."

"We need money, Hailey." Howie looked at Linda when she stood up and staggered to him. Holding her up, he watched her as she spoke to her daughter. "You did this. I hope that you have nightmares for the rest of your life for what you did to us. Had you just paid up and shut up, then we'd have our precious babies. They'd be right here with us instead of being in the morgue. I want to go and see them. now. And you're going to take us there."

"They've been buried. And the only place I'll take you is to your death if you ever fuck with me again. That is something you can bank on." Linda asked Hailey again for money. "Is that all you can think about? Money? For Christ's sake, did you not hear what I said? You murdered your children. You did this to them."

"No, no, that's not right. You were the one at fault here. You never was one to listen to your betters. It was all your fault. Every bit of this. And you're lying to me about them. You didn't have my permission to have anything done to them. So you take me to see them, or so help me, I'm going to blow your fucking brains out."

The gun—he'd forgotten that they had it—was pointed at Hailey as Linda laughed. It was crazy laughter. He had a feeling that Linda wasn't far from being with her kids, the way she was acting. If it wasn't by Hailey that she met her demise, then she'd do it herself. There was something very scary about her right now.

"Linda, honey, we'll go to see them. I think that you're right on that, she didn't have our permission to have them admitted to the hospital. That's where they're going to be, too. Aren't they Hailey? You fucking liar, tell us that you've lied to us for no good reason other than that you could."

When they turned and left the room, he stood there trying to figure out what had just happened. His kids—he knew that they were going to be all right. They'd only given them the heroin a few times while here. Yes, they had used it at home. They'd used it when they wanted to have sex or go out and have some fun. Surely that wouldn't be counted as giving them too much.

Linda screamed again, falling to the floor—the gun pointing at no one now—and gripping the paper like it was going to give her all the answers. Getting up, he took the paper from her and read the name of the funeral home. Going to the phone that no one used any more, he found the number and actually dialed it to reach someone of authority. Howie couldn't breathe around

159

the pain. He'd be better once someone told him that it had been all a lie.

The phone was answered with a brisk name of the funeral home. Howie made sure that the paper said that they'd all been at the same one, and tried to form a question to find out. Find out if any of this were true.

"My children were there. Someone told us that they were dead and that you have them. I don't believe for a minute that you would have them. Someone is keeping them from us. Tell me that you have no idea about them." The man asked him their names, and Howie had to think about that. His grief was so heavy that he couldn't think beyond this all being a cruel lie. Telling him all their names, the man said that he was sorry.

"No, you're not going to be sorry. You're going to tell me that you never heard of them. That that bitch Hailey lied to make us upset. You cannot have taken my children away from me." The phone slipped from his fingers when the man said again that he was sorry. But the Damon children, all three of them, were at peace now.

Howie had no idea how long he sat there, his mind not functioning right. He looked around the room and noticed that Linda had disappeared, but he wasn't worried. Howie was sure that she was going to come back and have the kids with her. And they'd climb in their old beater and go home. He was going to take care that they were all right from now on.

"No more drugs for them." He thought about something that Hailey had said to him, but let it go. "I'm not going to think about what she said. She's always been a liar, and I don't trust her any more now than I did when she was hanging around at our home."

Howie started packing up all their clothing, and the little

bear that Shelly would sleep with every night. He put that on top of the luggage—he was going to make sure that she had it first thing. When he'd taken their things out to the car, he came back inside to wait for Linda. He sat in front of the open door, wanting to see her and the children first thing. But as darkness began to take over the streets and put scary shadows in the room, he closed the door and laid down.

"I'll need to be fresh for the drive home."

Howie closed his eyes, but when images were there with Hailey and that man lying to him, he squeezed them tighter and thought of other things. Like when they were coming here and how upset he and Linda had been about the noise the kids were making. "It was only a little bit. There isn't any way that it hurt them as badly as she said. The cunt never did like me."

Opening his eyes, he saw that the room was bright with sunlight. Howie had never been one to be an early riser, but they had things to do today. They were leaving here, and he was never going to bring his family here again. This was not a place to bring children, where just anyone could tell lies about them.

It was nearing lunch time when he decided that he might have to go and find Linda. She was with their children, he knew that, so he was happy that they had their time together. But it was past time that they went home. So, he went to the bathroom to freshen up for her and saw her.

The gun lay on the toilet seat. Linda had put it there, he thought, just for him. The pink water hid her body from him, but he thought that was fine for now. The blood that was on the side of the tub and puddled on the floor, he told himself that she'd cut herself shaving her legs. She'd done it numerous times in their life together.

161

Howie picked up the gun to put it somewhere safe so that their kids couldn't find it. That would be terrible if one of them were hurt by it. He looked at the mirror that was over the sink and saw the three obituaries there. She'd plastered them to the mirror with the steam, he thought. It hit him then, hard and painfully, that his kids were gone. They were never going to pester him again. There would be no locking them in their room again so that he could have some quiet time with Linda.

Howie's grief was so strong and so painful that he sobbed from it, holding the gun to his chin as he sat there. There was only one way to end the pain. The only way that he was going to be able to be with his family again. Howie took hold of Linda's hand, so cold now in death, and pulled the trigger.

~*~

Colton hung up the phone and sat there for several minutes, just thinking. They were dead, found this morning when the motel employees heard a gunshot sometime earlier. He didn't know how to tell his new wife—they'd only gotten married that morning. When she came into his office, he reached for her and she backed from his extended hand. Before he could say anything to her, Hailey started talking.

"I would like to run with you. As a cat. I can do that—I've been practicing. It'll be fun, and we'll forget all the shit that has happened in the last forty-eight hours." He nodded and stood up. "I don't want you to tell me. It'll make it real, all right? I need this more than I would have thought possible. I want to run with you."

Colton followed her out to the deck. The fresh rain had done nothing to cool off the day; in fact, he thought it was hotter. Watching Hailey for any sign she was hurting, he smiled when she shifted to a beautiful cougar and took off running to the back of their property. Dad reached him just as he went from man to cat.

I'm assuming that you heard already. He said that he'd been called not ten minutes ago. *I thought so. How is Hailey taking it? I bet hard.*

I believe that she knows, but she asked me not to tell her, not yet. His dad said that he worried for her. *I think she's going to be fine, Dad. She's had what she needed in shoving them out of her life. There is a peace about her that I haven't seen since we came together. I think she's going to be just fine. In fact, we're running in the woods right now. You should see how beautiful her cat is.*

The two of you come over for dinner, if you would. The rest of them are going to be here, and I for one would like to have fun. Your mom is putting together an order for Chinese for us all, so I might need to borrow some money from you. Colton laughed when he saw Hailey leaping in the air like she was playing, like a small kitten. *You come over. I won't take no for an answer either. I've talked to Peter, and he's going to call his son to let him know, and they'll both be here as well.*

We'll be there, Dad. You let me know what time to get there, and Hailey and I will come over. She might need this and the run more than I've ever needed when I was hurting. Colton had lost a patient to suicide, and it was something that haunted him for months after, because the man had not gotten support from his family. Hailey would need that.

After closing the connection with his dad, he found himself searching for Hailey. She'd been here not a minute ago, and now he couldn't find her. Just as he was going by a large tree that had fallen in the last storm they'd had, she leaped out from behind it and tackled him to the ground. She and he shifted at the same time, him holding her in his arms when she came to him.

Kissing her, showing her how much he loved her, he moaned when Hailey sat up over him naked. Colton wanted her—had wanted her for so long it felt as if he'd been deprived of her. When he was as naked as she was, he helped her as she slid down over his cock, riding him slowly.

"You make me feel alive." He sat up to kiss her and she pushed him back down. "No, I need to feel like I'm doing something good. I don't know why sex came to mind, but you'll let me take you, won't you?"

"Yes, anytime you want." This time when he sat up, she let him. Nibbling on her breasts, he moaned when she wrapped her legs around him, and pulled her closer by cupping her ass. "Have you any idea how beautiful you are to me? To any person that sees you? Not just on the outside, but inside too, where it counts the most." She kissed him hungrily, and he returned it with as much as she was giving. "I need you. I want to make love to you here, in the woods."

Colton rolled her to her back, careful of anything that might hurt her. When she rolled her hips up to meet his, he took both her hands in his and held them over her head. He suckled at her breast, touched her everywhere he could with his free hand. Her moans were mingled with his own, a chorus that only the two of them could sing. Kissing her throat, then biting onto her ear lobe, Colton whispered how she tasted to him. How she felt wrapped around him. But most importantly, he told her how much he loved her.

When he finally let go of her hands, Hailey touched him, gave his body the same attention he'd given hers. Every whisper of her fingers over his skin brought it to life. Colton didn't want this to ever end, wished that they could hide away from the world and never have anything happen to them again.

When she kissed him again, she told him that she was ready. He smiled as he lifted her up by her ass and took all that she gave him. No matter what had happened or what would happen to them, he was in love with her, and that would make his world a much better place to live in.

Hailey cried out his name when she released. Colton watched her, knowing that there was still plenty of time to have his pleasure too. He made love to her with his mouth and hands while his body gave her what she needed. And when he was close, ready to fill her with everything that he was, she pulled him to her and let him take her one more time.

They laid there in the afterglow of making love. It wasn't as intense as they'd enjoyed before—it was slower, but it meant so much more to him. They were a couple, and as of earlier that morning, they were man and wife. Their life, to him, couldn't be any more complete.

"My parents want us to come over for Chinese food tonight. Everyone is going to be there, including your dad and brother." She looked at him and told him that was fine as she yawned around her words. They were dressed now, making their way back to the house. "What would you like to do in the meantime? I don't know about you, but I could use a nap. You've drained me dry, honey."

"He's not my father." Colton said that he knew that. "I knew that you did, but I wanted to say that he's not my father, but he never treated me as if I wasn't his. I never had a day when I was with him, before the divorce or after, that I ever felt like I wasn't of his body."

"Peter is a good man. And he loves you with all his heart. You know that, I'm sure." Hailey nodded and sat down on the porch swing that they'd only just gotten cleaned up. Rocking back and forth with her, he looked out over the pool and the trees to watch as the day slid away from them. "I've decided to quit my practice. I will continue to see people at the station houses that might need me, but I can't do the practice anymore. Not since you came into my life."

"I want us to adopt a child. I don't really care if it's a boy or girl, or even what nationality it might be. But I want to be there, as my father was for me, for someone that needs us." She looked at him, and he had a feeling that this was something that she'd been thinking about for some time. "We'll both be here for it. And any others that come into our lives. But our first child, I'd like for it to be someone that needs us, more than just a person to watch over as it grows up."

"I'm all for that. I'd love to have as many children as you'd like too. Anytime you wish." She nodded, and they rocked some more. His dad told him that dinner would be in an hour, and Colton told him that they'd be there. After telling Hailey what his dad said, she nodded and stood up.

"They're both dead, I know that." He told her he was sorry. "I am as well. I didn't like either of them, not at all, but they were a part of my life, and now they're gone too."

"I'll call tomorrow and have arrangements made for them." Colton stood up when she reached for him. "We'll just have a quiet service for them where only family will be there for you."

"Pete is going to move here. I'm going to make him." Colton didn't doubt one bit that she would. "I've missed him. He has a practice; he's an attorney that deals in estate planning. People trust him very much."

"I wouldn't doubt that he is as brilliant as you are." They were walking up the stairs to change as they spoke.

"Maybe you can convince Christian that he needs a partner."

"I've already set it up. They'll have a trial run, Christian said, but he knew that they were going to get along fine." Dressing slowly, touching one another any chance they got, she turned in his arms and laid her head on his chest. "Do you think it would be wrong of us to put them nowhere close to their children? I know that they can't really tell where they end up, but I don't want them by them. Not even in death."

"I agree with you. I think we can even arrange that they're in a separate cemetery." She said that she liked that. "Honey, are you all right? Is there anything that I can do for you?"

"You already have just by being who you are. I love you, Colton. I can't believe that it took me so long to figure that out. I'm so glad that you didn't give up on me." Colton told her never. "I'm glad. I love you."

"And I you."

When they arrived at his parents' house, the delivery person was just leaving. His brothers had helped him bring it all in—they'd made several trips, it seemed. Colton got to meet Pete, and saw that his father and he were just alike—both men of good standing, and people that he could like.

Dinner was just as he'd hoped it would be—loud and full of laugher, he and his brothers trying to outdo each other on outrageous antics. Mom and Dad laughed with them, Mom not even saying anything when they had a cursing contest. But it wasn't Dane or Hailey that won—it was his own dear mother. And the rest of the family was as shocked as he was.

"Well, hanging around the four of you has taught me a few things. Cursing is just one of the many habits I might just pick up."

Dad was still staring at Mom with his mouth open. His

167

family — there was never a quiet moment.

Chapter 13

Hailey turned to her class. "Anyone know the answer? Come on, guys, you've been studying this all year. What is the shape?" They all sat there as still as they could for sixth graders. "Okay then — Mary Stapleton, what is this shape?"

The little girl stood up, her hands gripped tightly together. "It's a rhombus?" Hailey asked her if that was her answer. "Yes. I think. I think it's a rhombus."

"Correct." She wrote the name of it on the board under the shape, then turned back to her class. "Everyone, let's give Mary an applaud."

Mary's face turned bright red, and Hailey moved to stand on the other side of her desk and sat on it. Reaching out, she knew that she'd upset the little girl, and that had not been her intentions.

"Mary knew the answer. I really want you to give her a hand." They did, but it was halfhearted. "All right. Why did I have you do that, does anyone know?"

Shawn, back row smart ass, raised his hand. After giving

him permission, he stood up and said his name, then answered. "You wanted to embarrass the crap out of her."

"No. I didn't have you try and embarrass her. You give someone a cheer because that's what you do when someone around you does a good job—you let them know. Guys, you have to celebrate the success of others around you to let them know that you're there for them." Every one of them seemed to be stretching their necks to get closer to her. "Let's say that Shawn is on the side of the road. It's dark and there aren't any lights or houses around. He has a flat tire and doesn't know how to change it. Mary comes along and helps you. And you thank her, right?"

"I can change a tire." Shawn got high fives from those around him. Hailey pointed out that they were cheering him on. "They like me."

"Of course they do. And you trust them, correct? When you're around them, if someone says a nasty comment to something, you congratulate them by the hand ritual. Right?" They were getting it. "Okay, so Shawn is at the side of the road and Mary stops. Two days before this, Shawn helped Mary pick up her books when they were knocked out of her hands. Does anyone know why he let her help him with the tire?"

"Because we trust him, even though I don't." Connie sat down and the girls around her did the same thing. "But you mean that he trusted Mary because he'd been there for her when she needed it. Like she was going to be there for him to change the tire."

"That's right. Now, Mary had the correct answer. What do we do to show her that we not just support her, but are also glad that it was her that I called on?" They all laughed, and she went back to the board. "All right. Can anyone tell me what this shape is?"

Hands were up everywhere, and Hailey made sure that each of them was called on. They were cheering one another on like they'd won the series in a four-straight playoff. When the bell rang for the next set of class mates to come in, Hailey did the exact same thing. By lunch, she'd seen four sets of kids, and every one of them went out standing a little straighter.

"You should have more control over your class, Miss Whitehead. That sort of behavior is what you send them to the principal's office for." Hailey was using her maiden name so that no one would associate her with the Stantons for this. She turned and looked at Steven White, her target for the day. "If you don't want to do that, just have me come in and I'll gladly show you how it's done."

"I encouraged them to have fun. Math is fun." He told her that it was disruptive. "To who? The kids are all participating. They're learning, and they are supporting each other in a way that makes them feel good about themselves, as well as others." He told her that was a good way to get herself fired. "Really? Well, if Mr. Henderson wants to come in and monitor my class, he's welcome. In fact, I'll invite him in. We'll see if he thinks what I'm doing is disruptive."

None of the other teachers in the lounge said anything; they kept their noses buried in whatever they were eating. Hailey knew why. Each of them, all the teachers here, knew what Steven was doing but had been threatened with harm to the children if they told. He had injured all of the children that belonged to these teachers, with the threat that there would be more injuries if they even thought about telling on him.

When the period was over for lunch, she went back to her classroom and got ready for the next group. She wasn't the least bit surprised that word had gotten around about her methods, and this class knew what to expect. Working on the shapes again, someone knocked on her door and she let the principal in. It was as if he brought a darkness over the room.

"Ladies and gentlemen, I'm sure you know the principal." They all nodded and didn't look his way. "I'm sorry, did you not hear what I said? Mr. Henderson is your principal. He's made it through school to be here today. Do you have any idea how much studying he had to do to be here for you? He is also the man that keeps you safe by getting extra funding so that there are new locks on all the doors."

The room erupted in applause, high fives, as well as a chorus of thanks from around the room. Turning back to the board, she continued with her lesson. The kids were like they'd been before he came in, supportive and happy. But best of all, they were learning.

At the end of the class, Mr. Henderson came up to her. She watched him carefully, but didn't say anything about her methods of teaching. So when he put out his hand, she took it in hers and smiled.

"They liked you." She said that she was trying to make that happen. "Yes, I got that. And I bet that if I were to quiz any one of them about shapes they just learned about, each of them would be correct. Thank you for this. You've brought a ray of happiness even into my day."

The rest of the afternoon was the same, and Mr. Henderson was there for every class after that. He said that he thought that they might see him in a different light rather than the man to come down on them.

Getting ready to go home, Hailey knew that she'd gladly do this every day. She'd been a teacher before and knew with certainty that it wasn't always like this. But it had been the kind that made her want to come into class every day and help kids.

Hailey was just putting her purse on her arm when Steven came into the room. Hailey wasn't alarmed—the entire room was not only bugged with microphones that could hear a fly fart but was also under camera surveillance. They were ready for him to make his move, and he would today, just so she was clear on things that he did right from the start.

Smiling at him, she put her purse down and looked at him. "I was just going home. Is there anything I can do for you? It is getting kinda of late, and my husband is waiting on me."

He slapped her, knocking her onto her desk. She could feel Colton's anger, and told him to just behave or she'd kick his ass.

He hit you. I'm going to kill him for that. She said that he was not. *You don't know what that feels like, to have you in there getting beat around while I'm out here in a nasty van.*

I do, too. Now leave me alone so we can get rid of this piece of shit.

Hailey sat up, holding her hand over her mouth because, like every other wound that she'd get, it was already healed. She backed a step away from Steven. "What was that for? What will my husband say when he sees this?"

"You want to be able to go home to your husband every night, Miss Whitehead? If you do, then you will do just what I tell you to do." Hailey nodded and asked him what he wanted. "You're going to come with me to my room, and once there, you're going to see that I'm not just a science teacher. And when we're done, you aren't going to say a word to anyone, or else you'll be out one husband."

Every room and hallway had been set up the way her classroom was, with cameras and microphones. Hailey walked ahead of him, still holding her mouth when Dane connected

173

with her. She and Hailey were the ones working with the Feds in taking this man off the street once and for all.

He's a nasty little fuck, isn't he? Hailey asked if Colton was all right. *He is now. I had to put a collar around his fucking huge neck and hog tie him, as Denny is so fond of saying. Do you suppose that when they're born, they have a head sitting on their shoulders because of the size of their necks? Never mind. That'll be a conversation we have later. But for now, Colton is being a very good boy. When you get to the room, don't be alarmed if you happen to see any of the men from yesterday in there. They're supposed to be hidden, but there isn't that much shit to hide behind in a lab. The fucker is going to be so surprised that I might just give him a high-five too.*

Hailey just caught herself from laughing. They were at his door now, where the Feds were. Late last night they'd gotten a look inside the room, and were amazed at how much equipment he had in there to have his own little out-in-the-open place to make drugs. She was standing at his work table when she saw the first guy.

You might want to tell the guy that is hiding in the closet that I can see his feet. Christ, they're huge too. Dane asked her if she'd heard that little saying about men and their feet when his feet were pulled back. *Yes, I have. And I can say with certainty that it's true. Colton wears a size thirteen, and there is absolutely nothing small about any of him. Now, hush, I'm going to get my first lesson in how to take a fucking asshole down.*

"Are you listening to me? Or do I have to show you who's the boss again?" She whimpered, and everyone listening in on their link laughed at her. She'd almost forgotten what she was doing. "Now, this is the way it's going to work. You're going to keep your mouth shut about anything that goes on around here. And, you fucking bitch, if you pull that clapping thing again, they'll never find your body. Do you hear me?"

"Yes, I do. But I don't understand about the goings on here. Are you still talking about my class?" She had to get him to admit it. Otherwise there wasn't any way they could convict him, because anyone could have put the drugs and related paraphernalia they'd found in his lab. "Please, don't hit me again."

"Didn't you hear? I'm the biggest drug lord there is in this fucking stupid little town. That's why no one has thought to look for me in this half-assed school. I make them right in here, and you're going to shut your fucking mouth or I will take care of you and that little husband of yours." Dane laughed in her head. "Now, this is what you're going to do for me, just so we're on the same page. You're going to take yourself a little of my high-grade product and snort it —"

The room seemed to explode with people coming in from everywhere. The Feds, armed and dangerous, had Steven down on the floor and were reading him his rights. When he was cuffed and taken away, he was still screaming at her that he was going to make her pay. Hailey had a seat on the closest chair and frowned. That was entirely too easy, she thought.

"It's done." She nodded at Dane when she came to sit by her. "You did well with this. And with teaching. The kids will remember you well after they graduate from here."

Hailey looked at her. "While I do thank you for the compliment, I have a feeling that there is a *but* attached to it somehow. What are you trying very hard not to tell me or ask me? I have to go home and take a shower. I feel nasty after that." Dane stood up and she did as well. "Well, tell me or I go looking for it."

"The school's board of directors — which includes Denny, by

the way — wants you to stay and teach. I guess Mr. Henderson asked for and received a copy of your earlier classes and called an emergency meeting for them to beg you to stay. You made such a difference with most of those kids that their next class was so much easier for the other teachers." Dane put up her hand and Hailey gave her a smack on it. "Say you'll do it, and even I will be grateful to you. With our own kids coming to this family, I'd like to know that you're going to be here for them."

Colton joined her then, taking her hand in his and kissing it. "I don't know what to say about that, Dane. I really don't. While I love teaching and I had a wonderful time today, I think that they'll soon grow tired of me. Because you know me well enough — I'm not going to be just a teacher here. I'd be an advocate for their wellbeing, too."

"Good. I'll tell them you're taking it." Dane walked away from her and Colton, and she turned to him when he began laughing.

"I think I just took the position here. How did that happen?" Colton was still laughing when he told her that they were headed to dinner with the family. "Are they going to tell me to take it too?"

"Oh honey, you can count on that. And I'll put in my vote for you to do it too."

Somehow, she didn't think that voting was going to be necessary. Dane was going to have her working here first thing in the morning. And Hailey wasn't really upset about it.

~*~

Ray hung up the phone and glanced around her office — not really looking for anything, just thinking. She was in a great deal of pain right now but talking to David for the last twenty minutes had made her day. All she had to do was make the necessary arrangements and she'd be with him in two days.

Sitting up slowly so as not to tear into any of the stitches, she made her way to the little fridge that currently had more food in it than the one at home did. Ray even had a small cot in the other room that she'd take a nap on when things were stressful at work.

"Like that isn't always going on." Ray winced when she bent over to grab a candy bar, her usual supper of late. She knew that this was more than just a deadline that she was trying to hit, but her father was making things difficult for her about the will that Grandma had left.

The old bird had put her before the firing squad, so to speak. And if she had known that her grandma had a thriving business that Ray was now in charge of too, she might not have sent her anything over the years.

"Yes, I would have. She was my world." Going back to her desk with a second candy bar, she munched on the first one while she thought about the will and everything else that had happened since Grandma had passed away. Picking up the phone again, she made all the necessary arrangements to go to her little brother. She needed to see him.

Working late hadn't ever been something that she'd shied away from. It was what had gotten her where she was today. Seventy-five stores around the country that sold her furniture. There were seven more slated to take her on over the next three years. Ray had worked very hard to get to the point where she was today, and still worked too.

The plan for the table that she was working on was giving her fits. Pulling out sheets of stock paper, she cut out the pattern that she'd used and then built it into the blueprints for it. This was what she did to work out flaws and other issues.

She knew there was a program on her computer that she could have used to do this very thing, but she liked getting her hands dirty, so to speak. When the table was built by what she'd done, there she found the missing element to make it work for her. When her phone rang right in the middle of her adjusting things on both the blueprint and her mock up, she reached for it without looking to see who it might be.

"I hear you're coming to town soon." Smiling, she told Hailey that she was leaving on Thursday, just two days away. "Great. I hope that you make time to come and see me. I have been so busy lately with all the crap that's going on around here."

"I read about your parents. I'm so sorry, Hailey. Is there anything I can do for you?" Ray had also read the three obituaries for the children, and that had broken her heart.

"Nah, just having you come here is good enough for me. We, none of us, got along at all, so it's not as hard as I'd thought it would be. Actually, it's sort of a relief." Hailey laughed, and Ray wondered if she should too. "When I say that we didn't get along, that's an understatement. They went out of their way to make me dislike them for a lot of years. And with the kids being hurt by them, it was all I could do not to hunt them down myself. Enough about that. Have you had any more trouble from your own dad?"

"Yes, probably as much as you have with yours before this. He's really pissed off that when the will was read, he found out that Grandma had been holding out on him. Honestly, it startled me as well. She was the head of the board on several companies. But she owned a lot of them too." Hailey said that she'd bet that Ray was now the owner and the head of several companies. "Yes, you have that right. And they're worth more than I thought. I've been going over the books to them, just to see where we are, and that takes me away from what I want to do. Design."

"I've recently been talked into becoming a teacher. The hardest part of the job is not cursing. There are days when I want to say to one of them, 'What the fuck is wrong with you?' But alas, I can't do that. Nor can I shake the shit out of them." They both laughed, and Ray hurt herself and moaned at the pain. "When did he knock you around this time? Recently, I bet."

Ray, for the first time in her adult life, unburdened herself on a near stranger. Crying hard, she told her what he'd said to her just before he caught her in the parking garage alone.

"I did everything I could to try and hit back, even going so far as to spray pepper spray on him. But he had me at a disadvantage. I swear, he wants to kill me. I don't know what I can do about this." Hailey had a suggestion. "Yes, while killing him might give me some peace, it would be from a prison cell, and I'm not that far gone yet."

Hailey had called her several times over the last few weeks, just when she needed someone to joke with—a much needed smile that she got when she'd told her a story about her new life. For some reason Hailey had clicked with her, and had enjoyed her phone calls as well as her emails.

"When you get here, we'll make a plan. I know how much you like plans. And we'll call the others in on this. I'm warning you again, Dane is scary. I am too now, but she is really scary. And the other women that I've come to love, they're just as mean when cornered as the rest of us are." Hailey laughed, and then asked her again when he'd knocked her around. "I have things to tell you about what I've been changed into. Some of it

179

is that I can see how you're feeling."

"You told me that Dane is the one that did this to you. I wonder if I paid her enough, if she'd do the same to me. I don't know how much more I can take of this." Ray cried again, reaching for the tissues just out of her reach. When the box fell to the floor, Ray leaned out of her chair to get it.

The door to her office opened slowly. The lights were all off except the one on her desk, so whoever it was, she hoped that they'd' think she was gone and leave too. Or it could have just been the cleaning crew coming in. But she didn't think her luck would be that good.

"Don't speak. Just listen to me, Ray. I'm going to come for you." She nodded into the phone as she tried to get out of her chair without making any noise. "It's your father. I want you to scream as loudly as you can. The cleaning crew is one office door down from you, and they'll hear you. But wait until I can get them to turn off their headphones."

Her fear was making her sick. If he found her, there was no telling what he'd do to her this time. Ray had a fleeting moment to wonder how Hailey could tell her all this, but didn't care, so long as she could come out of this on the other side.

"He's looking around for things to destroy. Just stay were you are. Help is coming. It might be a little later than I want—you're going to be hurt, but I'm getting you help." Ray nodded again just as the noise of broken glass shattered the silence of the room. When the chair was suddenly pulled back from the desk, she knew she was going to die. "No, you're not. Scream, Ray—scream like your life depends on it. Because honey, it does."

Dad grabbed her by the leg and pulled her out from under the desk. She'd almost forgotten that she had the phone still in her hand when she heard Hailey tell her to scream. Taking in as much air as she could with her broken ribs, she let loose a cry that she was sure would wake the dead.

He hit her with his fist in the face and belly. Ray kept screaming through it all, praying that Hailey was right, help was coming. When he hit her with something hard in the face, she went down just as her dad disappeared from in front of her. She looked at the wolf that was grappling with Dad and closed her eyes. Every part of her was hurting, and she knew that she wasn't going to make it.

She must have passed out, because when she heard voices telling her to open her eyes, she swung out with her fist and connected. The person held her painfully until she understood what he was saying. Help. He was there to help her. Trying to sit up, the voice told her to lay back.

"I've called an ambulance. They're on their way. I was told not to move you, but if I could get you to tell me your name." She tried to think, but it was too painful—she wanted to curl into a ball and die. "Hailey—you know her—she said to tell you that you'd fucking better not die on her, she's looking forward to your visit. Tell me your name and we'll all feel better."

"Rachel. Ray Spencer. Where is he? Don't let him near me, please." She still couldn't open her eyes. "What's wrong with me? I can't open my eyes. Did he hurt me?"

"Yes." That was all he said for a few moments. She didn't dare ask him again—she thought perhaps she didn't want to know. "Your face is pretty battered up, Ray. You have a bad cut on your face that looks like you might need fifty or so stitches to repair it. Do you want me to go on?"

"No, that's enough for now. I can talk and think. The rest is...can wait. Am I blind now? Did he do something that will make me blind?" He didn't speak, and she could hear him talking to someone else. She was touched, and Ray screamed again at the pain. "Please, don't leave me. I don't know who you are or where you came from, but don't leave me."

"They're going to give you something for pain. Hailey said that you're not allergic to anything, right?" She said no, she wasn't. Ray was trying to get her mind wrapped around what he wasn't telling her. "No, you're not blind. But you are badly hurt around your eyes. Hailey, she said to tell you that you'll be fine now, and that she's coming for you."

"She's my only friend. Tell her that I'm so grateful to her for helping me." The stranger, he said that she could hear her. "I don't know how you're doing this, Hailey, but you can have anything I have for keeping me from dying."

"You're going to feel a pinch, Ray. And when you do, you have to let the drugs take you. If you don't, if you fight them, you're going to be awake when they have to move you to the gurney. All right?" She asked him what his name was. "I'm Danny Miller. I'm the alpha around here."

The drugs were taking her under, and she was a little fuzzy about what was being said. Ray knew shifters—she had two working for her. But she wasn't sure how this man was talking to her and Hailey couldn't.

I'm here. I didn't want you to freak out more right then. You did good, my friend. And I'm coming for you. Just let them take care of you and you'll be all right. I have the best there is there for you. She could hear her and asked her if she was really alive. *Yes, you're alive. But your father isn't. I'm sorry. Danny had to kill him to get him to stop hurting you.*

I don't care. Ray, on some level, knew that they were talking through some kind of link to each other. The drugs were taking her under, and she had one more thing to tell Hailey. *She'll come now. And she's worse than my father.*

We'll be ready.

Chapter 14

Hailey had never been in a private jet before. She knew that it would be a nice ride, but what she didn't expect, and probably should have, was that it was so fucking huge. With only the three chairs that were in the middle of the room and a desk with a phone in one corner, it was spacious. She supposed that all planes were this big; she'd just never thought of what it looked like empty like this.

"We'll be there in about thirty minutes." She nodded at Colton, so glad that he was able to come with her. The police departments had heard that he retired from his practice, and thought that meant that he was free to come to them more. "I've gotten some updates, as I'm sure you have. She's doing well now. The surgery should be over by the time we land."

"I've talked to Danny. One of his pack is the surgeon. I could talk to him too, I guess, but I want him to have his full attention on what he's doing." Colton nodded and picked her up off her chair and sat her down on his lap. "Much better. I'm so worried about her. And when her aunt finds out that Alan is

185

dead, I'm assuming that you know that we're going to have to protect Ray."

"Yes, I have high hopes that she does come around and try to fuck with us." Colton laughed.

"Ray was so afraid that it was impossible to talk to her through the link when he was in her office. I'm so glad that she kept the phone with her during this. Otherwise I wouldn't have been able to help her as I did."

"I am as well. I've also spoken to Danny. He said she's in bad shape. He doesn't think we'll be able to have her moved for a few days." She looked at Colton. "David said he *didn't think* we could, but we know better. The back end is ready for anything that she needs. Dad is back there now making sure that it's all in place and ready. Even Wyatt said that he was astonished at how quickly you were able to get this in place."

"The power of friendship." He nodded, and she leaned back on him. "Her face is really a mess. She is going to need a lot to put her back together. Mentally and physically, I think. Danny said that Alan had used a knife on her, and also the arm of her chair. I'm glad he's dead. If he hadn't of been, I would have gladly taken him out."

Hailey thought about what she knew of Ray's injuries. Her right arm was broken in two places, and her left hand had been shattered when Alan had tried to grind it into the carpet. He'd taken the cradle of the phone and beaten her face until it was nothing more than a bloodied mess.

Her right eye was swollen shut and would need a lot of stitches to repair the flesh around it. The left eye socket had been broken and may need additional surgeries to get it to look better. Both lips were stitched up—seven on the upper, ten on the lower. Ray would need lots of help and a great deal of care.

"Do you suppose that she's one of the others' mates?" She told Colton that she'd not thought of that. "I have since you mentioned her a while back. You and she are friends, you met under odd circumstances, and now this."

"I guess when we get there, Wyatt will be the first to test your theory." She thought of Ray and what she would need when this was finished. "I actually hope that she is Levi's mate. They both seem to be so tender, and yet strong enough to fight back when necessary. His art is very telling, don't you think?"

"I've not seen any of it since he got out of college. Well, that's not true. I have seen it, but not personally. I have to look it up online when I want to see his work. He's very close mouthed about it." Hailey nodded, and the pilot said that they were ten minutes from landing. "How did you manage to see any of it, when the rest of us couldn't?"

"Levi talks to me. He and I have a good relationship. But rather than being close mouthed about what he does, I think he's fighting with shyness." Hailey got into her seat and buckled in to land. "When we get there, David is going to meet us at the landing strip. He and his pack have been protecting her since they took her in. They know Caroline all too well, I guess."

She was a horror, Hailey had figured out. When she'd taken a walk through Ray's mind, she'd found all kinds of things about her aunt that she was sure few people knew about. But the thing that had surprised her most was that Caroline and Alan never spoke to one another. David hadn't even been aware that he had an aunt until she asked him about her.

"Dane is looking into things for you. She said that she's not finding much, and that bothers her on so many levels. There is no mention of her in the obit for Alma, nor on any of the paperwork from the attorneys. Christian said that he has an idea and is going to go that route. Do you suppose that she's not really an aunt?" Hailey told him that Ray thought she was, so that's all she'd been able to find out about her. "So, you can't do that mind thing and find her through a connection. Don't you think that is odd too?"

"Are you kidding me? Odd? What I think is odd is that I can do it in the first fucking place. All I need to do is think of someone, or even hear about someone, and poof, I have everything I've ever wanted to know about them. Even what sort of sex life they prefer." She shivered when she thought of Steven White and his sexual activities. Colton laughed. "Yes, laugh it up, buddy. But be aware that with this odd shit going on in my head, I know your parents' sex life too."

"Eww, that's gross." She laughed. "Don't tell me that. Now all I can think about is they actually have sex. I mean, I know that they do, otherwise we'd not be here. But I don't want you to give me one detail. Not one."

"I'm going to use that one on Brayden the next time he gives me shit." Colton asked her if she really did have access to that. "Oh yeah. I mean, this is seriously some fucked up shit that I can do. You should try it sometime."

"Oh no. Oh, hell no. I do not now, nor do I ever want to go there. With anyone. Not one little bitty detail." She told him that his dad liked to be on top. "Mother fuck, Hailey. Did you not just hear what I said?"

"I'm joking with you. Just how do you think Brayden will take it?" Colton said that he wanted to be there when she did it to him. He might even record it for use later. "I'll do it when he least expects it."

The plane landed without any trouble. Both Wyatt and Denny were going to stand by in the family owned jet just to make sure that everything was ready for their patient. Taking the limo that was there for their use, Danny joined them. He caught them up on what he'd been able to find out, which was nothing.

"I have several of the pack watching both her office and her apartment. Rachel doesn't have that much of a staff working for her, but then the place is small. Even the fridge is small and empty." Colton thanked him and said that he'd make a donation to the pack for helping them. "Thank you. We're having some issues—nothing that we can't overcome, but they are draining the bank, so to speak."

"I'll be glad to help you in any way. What you did for us and for Ray, I won't ever forget that." Danny nodded. She could tell that he was embarrassed to say something like that to them, but he was getting desperate, and she wanted to help them with that.

After telling Colton how bad things were in the pack, he told her that he'd take care of it. She had no doubt that he would, too. As soon as they pulled up in front of the hospital, she could see the extra staff around, as well as a few people carrying guns. Danny was taking this very seriously. Hailey thanked him again for that.

Ray was out of surgery when she asked at the desk. The nurse was extremely helpful, telling them that she was in recovery but the doctor would be out to talk to them. Hailey had told everyone that Ray was her sister, and was all she had. No one questioned that, and she was able to get what she needed.

The doctor joined them later. He sat down, and she could see that he was exhausted. The surgeries on Ray had taken six hours, and there had been three different surgeon's working at the same time with her body.

"She's out of surgery, but I have her sedated pretty heavily. I'm to understand that you're taking her home with you today." Colton said that in addition to Hailey, Ray had a little brother back where they lived. "I'm glad to tell you the truth. Miss Spencer is going to need a lot of help when she gets out of this. And a great deal of support from family. The woman is lucky to be alive. Had it not been for Danny.... Well, let's just say that she'd not have gotten as far as she did."

Hailey knew that Danny had given her a bit of himself. Being an alpha, his blood was powerful. Not as much as hers, nowhere near that, but the boost to her system had helped. Again, she was grateful to the alpha.

He told them what she'd already found out about Ray. The surgery had repaired a lot of her injuries, but she was far from out of the woods. Asking to be excused, Hailey went to see if she could sneak in and see her. At the very least, she wanted to be there if she needed her.

Colton asked her if she was all right when he found her at the nursery looking in the big window. Hailey told him that she'd not been able to get even close to the recovery room, but had touched her mind.

"She's resting well. I just came here when I needed a pick-me-up." There were six babies on display in the little room — four little girls and two boys, if their little hats were any indication. "When I see these little guys, it makes me hurt more about those other children. I know that we couldn't have done any more for them, but at times, I feel as if I failed them somehow."

"Don't do that, Hailey. You did everything you could to help them, and when it was obvious that they were going to pass on, you made sure that they weren't alone when they did. I don't think anyone could have done any more for them under the circumstances." It still hurt her. "I've been looking into the adoption agencies around the area. You'll be happy to know that they're all ready and willing to give us any number that we want in children, even going so far as to give us a years' worth of diapers if we do. I think they're slightly overwhelmed at the present."

"When do we go and fill out the applications?" Hailey watched a nurse as she changed a diaper on one of the little girls. "I hope your mom was serious when she said that she'd be there for us. I don't have a clue how to raise a baby."

"You'll be just fine." He pecked on the window between them and the babies and showed the nurse his identification. It proclaimed him to be a doctor, and she nodded when she went to the door so that they could enter. "My wife would like to help you out. Can she take one of them and feed it for you?"

Hailey was suddenly thinking this was a terrible idea, and wondered what the hell he was thinking. But as soon as she was gowned up and sat in a rocker, the little bassinet was brought to her. The nurse told her how to hold her to feed her, and handed the baby to her.

Her little tiny mouth made Hailey's heart melt when she puckered it up. "She's going to be adopted as soon as the family gets their home ready. Their paperwork is all filed for her. They are so excited to have her come to them." Hailey nodded as she put the little nipple of the bottle at the little girl's mouth. "Two of the other children here are also being adopted. The others are going home with family."

Hailey had needed this. The child's mind was clear of any wrong doing. She'd not had anything to scare her or to make her upset, so she was, for her age, a very contented little baby. When she held her to burp her, Colton took his turn holding her.

"Thank you for this." He said that it was his pleasure. "You're very good to me, Colton. You make me love you more and more every minute of every day."

"And I love you as well, my love." The baby was given back to the nurse, who thanked them several times for helping them out. Going to wait for the okay to take Ray home with them, neither of them spoke.

They had a long road ahead of them, Hailey knew that. But for now, things were calm enough that she could take a breath, plan her next move, and rest for whatever came.

At just after six that morning, Ray was being loaded into the jet and readied for coming home. Wyatt told them that she wasn't his mate.

Damn it. Well, Hailey thought, there was one more. Perhaps, hopefully, Ray would be Levi's mate after all.

~*~

Levi worked on the canvas for another hour. He didn't care much for it, and finally, after playing with it for too long, he stopped what he was doing and took a break. There was no reason for him to hurry though this particular painting, but he was trying to keep his mind busy, and painting usually worked. He both wanted it over with and not coming up on what was making him insane. The judges were arriving in two weeks to see if his things were right for the upcoming Prestige Art Award.

The PAA, as they called it, was only given out once every two years. This year he'd been chosen to be one of the five candidates that were picked from around the world. Along with his name being in every paper around the world and his name inscribed on the walls in their headquarters as a winner, he'd get an actual award, as well as a ten thousand dollar gift.

It was a big deal, these people picking him. He'd had the nod to be one of the alternates once before, but they had picked a different five. Easily, Levi thought. He wanted this award more than he did the others that he'd won. However, he didn't want it for all the hoopla that went with it. He was, and always had been, a loner. And someone that would get ill if he was in the limelight.

Levi glanced over at the closet that was off limits to everyone. The lock on it would keep out only the less determined person, but no one came in here except him and the man who helped by cleaning up. He only looked in there when he had something to add to it. Going there now, he opened the door and put the newspaper clipping on the shelf. Then he stood back and really stared at the contents.

There were dozens of trophies from all the art shows, from childhood to now, that he'd ever attended. There were copies of checks, award money that he'd won too, which he'd donated to the local school as a teachers' helper fund. And they would get this one if he won, so long as they kept up their agreement to never say who it was from. Every clipping of every paper that talked about his work was there, some of them in different languages, papers that he'd gotten and treasured in his own way. For him.

Closing up the door and securing it, he looked at the entrance to his place and nearly let his cat go, he was so shocked. Whoever he'd expected to be there, it wasn't his mom. Closing the door and the lock, he smiled at her and hugged her tightly. His mom wasn't like other moms he knew. She was kind and loving, and would kick your ass all the way home if you messed up.

"What are you doing out here when you should be enjoying the sunshine? You need to come out sometimes, or people will think you're a vampire." They both laughed, and he led her away from his work. But she wasn't having it. "What are you hiding away from me? I'm your mother, you know, and no matter your age, young man, I can still take you to the woodshed."

"Yes, I know that you of all people can do that. But it's my… just, it's things that are better left unsaid. At least for me." She stared at him for several minutes, literally five, then turned out of his embrace and went to the door that he'd just locked. "Mom, please don't do this. It's nothing, really."

"If I believed that I wouldn't be thinking of dead bodies, military grade weapons, or sex toys. Actually, if there are sex toys in there, I don't want to know. But I know that it's not, because you would have told me that because you'd want me to defend you should someone say something." Mom put her arms over her chest and tapped her foot, a sure sign that she wasn't budging. "Open the door, Levi, or I'll have Dane come here and pick the lock."

He didn't want to. Levi was sure as he stood there that she'd want to make a big deal about it. But she'd also not leave here, and would do just what she said she would if he didn't.

Going to the door, he took out his key and shoved it into the lock. He was angry, but he didn't know at who right now. His mom for making him do this, or him because he was so determined that no one knew.

When it was unlocked, he turned to look at her. She looked as if she was regretting what she'd done. When he walked away, going home, Levi didn't say a word to her. If she looked or not, it was out of his hands. He only hoped that she'd see it, lock the door, and walk away.

Before You Go...

HELP AN AUTHOR

write a review

THANK YOU!

Share your voice and help guide other readers to these wonderful books. Even if it's only a line or two your reviews help readers discover the author's books so they can continue creating stories that you'll love. Login to your favorite retailer and leave a review. Thank you.

AWARD WINNING, BESTSELLING AUTHOR

Kathi Barton, winner of the Pinnacle Book Achievement award as well as a best-selling author on Amazon and All Romance books, lives in Nashport, Ohio with her husband Paul. When not creating new worlds and romance, Kathi and her husband enjoy camping and going to auctions. She can also be seen at county fairs with her husband who is an artist and potter.

Her muse, a cross between Jimmy Stewart and Hugh Jackman, brings her stories to life for her readers in a way that has them coming back time and again for more. Her favorite genre is paranormal romance with a great deal of spice. You can visit Kathi online and drop her an email if you'd like. She loves hearing from her fans. aaronskiss@gmail.com.

Follow Kathi on her blog: http://kathisbartonauthor.blogspot. com/